LUCY DANIELS

Hamster
— *in a* —
Hamper

Illustrations by Shelagh McNicholas

Hodder
Children's
Books

a division of Hodder Headline plc

Special thanks to Jenny Oldfield.
Thanks also to C. J. Hall, B.Vet.Med., M.R.C.V.S., for reviewing
the veterinary information contained in this book

Text copyright © Ben M. Baglio 1996
Created by Ben M. Baglio
London W6 0HE
Illustrations copyright © by Shelagh McNicholas 1996

First published in Great Britain in 1996
by Hodder Children's Books
This edition published in 1997

A Catalogue record for this book is available from the British Library

ISBN 0 340 62010 2

Typeset by Avon Dataset Ltd, Bidford-on-Avon B50 4JH

Printed and bound in Great Britain by
Clays Ltd, St Ives plc

Hodder Children's Books
a division of Hodder Headline plc
338 Euston Road
London NW1 3BH

One

Mandy Hope sat with her chin cupped in both hands. She was daydreaming in class, while sun streamed in through the biology lab window. Miss Temple was handing back the homework books. Mandy gazed at Henry the Eighth, the school hamster, treading steadily inside his exercise wheel.

Henry the Eighth was a good name, she decided. Like all hamsters, Henry had a funny habit of pouching his food in his cheeks, which puffed out, making him look enormously fat and self-important. His golden brown whiskers and the flash of white on the chest completed his resemblance to the famous king of England.

Treadle-treadle-rattle-spin went the wheel. Henry's squat little legs trotted on. Mandy smiled absent-mindedly. Henry was the eighth and last hamster in his litter, hence his name. Miss Temple had found homes for all the rest, but had decided to keep Henry as the school pet. She said he was a hamster with attitude. Mandy supposed this meant that he had a cheeky glint in his enormous dark eyes. Anyway, Henry had turned into one of the friendliest little animals, happy to sit in your hand nibbling dry porridge oats or to take a small chunk of brown bread and hold it delicately between his front paws.

And that was the problem; he was too friendly and too greedy. Everyone who came up to his cage for a chat slipped him a few goodies. He gobbled crisps, sandwich crusts, apple cores. You name it, Henry ate it. And he was fat!

He had a nice life though, sitting inside his airy wooden cage on the sunniest ledge in the biology lab, alongside the geraniums and the spider plants. He'd put on weight, and no amount of treading the exercise wheel seemed to take it off again. Podgy, pouchy, overweight little Henry weighed in at a mighty one hundred and fifty grammes. He was a heavyweight hamster. Mandy smiled and dreamed on.

HAMSTER IN A HAMPER

Mandy caught James's eye. 'Can I guess what you're thinking?'

'I'm thinking fresh vegetables, dried oats, nuts and rusks!'

'No more crisps?' She began to smile. 'James, you're planning to put Henry on a diet!'

'A calorie count,' he confirmed.

'A strict regime.'

'An exercise plan, so we can bring him back in September looking like a new hamster. No more excess fat.' He grinned.

'Poor Henry.' Mandy shook her head. 'I suppose it's for his own good, though.'

'Poor Henry, nothing! My house is going to be the first hamster health farm in the country!'

'Mandy Hope.' Miss Temple's voice brought her back to earth. 'Hello, Mandy. Knock, knock, is anybody there?' She came up to Mandy's bench and rattled her knuckles against it, exercise book at the ready. 'Don't you want to know your homework grade?'

Mandy blushed and pushed her blonde hair behind her ears. 'Sorry.' Sheepishly she took her book.

'Don't worry. Only one more day to go before we break up!' Miss Temple's smile was warm and friendly. 'You're not the only one who can't wait for the end of term.'

This time Mandy grinned. She liked the biology teacher, and this wasn't just because biology was her favourite school subject, with all the fascinating facts about animals. Miss Temple herself was bright and young; quite strict when she wanted her pupils to pay attention, but open to a joke and a kind word. She didn't look like a teacher either, with her wavy brown hair straying out of its ponytail and her light summer dresses.

'I was watching Henry doing his workout,' Mandy explained.

Miss Temple glanced at her watch and told the class to pack away their things. 'Ah, our dear little

Mesocricetus auratus! That's his official, scientific name.' She smiled, glancing at Henry. 'Or not so little, as the case may be. He could really do with being put on a strict diet. And that reminds me.' She walked back to the front of the class and clapped her hands for attention. 'Listen for a moment, everyone!'

Mandy watched a couple of people in the front row having a whisper and a giggle behind their hands. End-of-term fever was really setting in. One girl, Vicki Simpson, had gone bright red and sat on the edge of her seat. She watched Miss Temple step up the ledge towards her own demonstration bench. Vicki's friend, Becky Severn, dug her in the ribs and warned her to be quiet. Meanwhile, Vicki's twin brother, Justin, retreated from Miss Temple's bench, a wide grin spread across his round, freckled face.

Miss Temple clapped again and the room fell silent. 'I want to make an announcement before the bell goes.' She paused and cocked her head to one side. She listened hard. 'What's that noise?'

In the silence, Mandy could hear Henry plodding steadily inside his wheel. *Treadle-treadle-rattle-spin*. 'It's Henry, Miss!' she volunteered, pointing him out to the teacher.

But Miss Temple frowned. 'No, not that.

Something else; a kind of whirring sound.' She leaned across her bench towards the board duster, carelessly scrunched and pushed to one side.

Mandy saw Justin's grin expand. Vicki's face was ready to explode into laughter.

Miss Temple peered at the red checked duster. The faint whirring sound was definitely coming from under there. Gingerly she poked the duster, then raised a tiny corner. The whirring grew louder, like an angry bee.

Miss Temple gritted her teeth. She lifted the duster clear of the bench. A round, fat, hairy thing with eight long, spindly legs shot out from under it. Mandy stared wide-eyes. The 'thing' was a giant spider; a noisy, buzzing, creeping, squelchy, hairy-legged spider.

Vicki Simpson jumped to her feet for a better view. Becky held her back. Justin jumped on to his seat. The whole class was in uproar!

The spider shot across the bench, whirring angrily. It scrabbled across the length of the teacher's workbench and came up against a tall pile of textbooks, where it whirred and flailed.

'Hmm.' Miss Temple put on her best science teacher's voice. 'I suspect it's *Arachnis dunlophobia*, a very rare species indeed.' She poked at the spider with the sharp end of a pencil. It turned and sprinted back along the bench. A squeal shivered round the class.

Mandy squinted hard at the creature. Its grey, bumpy body was covered in ugly yellow blotches. It had big red eyes. Its legs, those long, hairy things, moved like clockwork. *Ah!* She caught Miss Temple's eye. *Clockwork,* she thought.

'Now, everyone, calm down and stand back. Justin, get down from that chair, please,' the biology teacher ordered. She went straight to the high shelf behind her desk and brought back a large, empty glass jar. 'I want to take this specimen alive.' Swiftly she trapped the spider inside the jar. A muffled whirring emerged. Legs scrambled helplessly against the glass. The spider tumbled and rolled. Then the whirring slowed and faded to a stop.

'Is it dead, Miss?' Justin demanded. He grinned at his twin sister.

Miss Temple winked at Mandy. 'No, Justin. *Arachnis dunlophobia* is a tougher species than that!' Carefully she lifted the jar and picked up the spider between thumb and forefinger. 'In fact, if we just wind this little knob here, I expect we'll soon revive him, no problem!' She smiled as she wound up the rubbery toy and placed him right way up on the bench once more. Sure enough, the spider began charging in straight lines up and down the bench.

'Oh!' Becky Severn sat back in her seat and fanned herself. 'It's a trick!' Vicki bit her lip, waiting to see how the teacher would react. Only Justin remained calm. Mandy saw him, standing hands in pockets, the grin fixed on his sturdy face.

Miss Temple raised her eyebrows at him. 'What a pity, Justin. I thought we were on to an exciting scientific discovery there. A Nobel prize at the very least.'

Justin kept on grinning. But when Miss Temple took the toy spider and placed it, legs still whirring away, inside her drawer, his smile began to fade. 'Hey, Miss, that's my spider!' he complained.

She cut him short. 'Yes, Justin, I know perfectly well it's *your* spider. But I think I'll just keep an eye on him for the rest of the day, if you don't mind. Now, you can make yourself nice and useful.' She picked up the duster and thrust it towards him in a cloud of chalk. 'Why don't you clean the board for me while I make my announcement? I'll have a word with you during break, *after* the bell has gone.'

Justin's mouth turned down, but Miss Temple had the upper hand. She hadn't panicked; she'd turned the joke against him. She waited until Justin settled into his task, then turned to the rest of the class.

Good for you, Mandy thought. Justin was well known as a loud-mouth and a bully. But Miss Temple had handled him well. She saw his twin sister sit back in her place, head down, unwilling to make eye contact. Gradually everyone settled down.

'It's about Henry,' Miss Temple began. 'We need to find him a good home for the school holiday.' A murmur ran round the room. The teacher raised both hands, asking for quiet. 'We need someone who can collect the cage after school tomorrow, take it home and look after him for six weeks. That means, preferably someone whose family is not going on holiday themselves, whom we can rely on to change the bedding every day, make sure that Henry gets his exercise and food, and a bit of regular company.' She paused while people considered this.

Mandy sighed and gazed at Henry. He'd stopped exercising and come out on to the floor of his cage to groom. His lovely marmalade-coloured coat shone in the sun. He stared back at her with his short sighted, twinkling dark eyes. His nose and whiskers twitched. *If only*, she thought. Looking after Henry for the summer would be fantastic. But it was out of the question. As vets at Animal Ark, her mum and dad had a rule that they would never take in extra animals; not strays, nor friends' cats and dogs, nor orphans from the wild. 'We're not a boarding-kennels, Mandy. We're vets,' her mum would say, kindly but firmly. 'No extra responsibilities, remember. We have enough as it is.'

Mandy reluctantly admitted that her mum and dad were right never to break their rule.

'This person must take great care to feed Henry his proper diet; cereal, rusks, nuts, fruit and vegetables, and not too many snacks!' Miss Temple paused to make the point about Henry's weight problem, then went on. 'There must always be clean drinking water in his cage. And you must be

especially careful to keep it locked tight at night.
Night-time is when pet hamsters get up to their tricks
if you let them.

'So it's a responsible job, but if you feel you would
like to have a go at looking after Henry, please write
your name on a piece of paper as you go out of the
lab. I'll take in all the names and put them into a
hat. The one I draw out will be the lucky caretaker.
I plan to make the draw early tomorrow morning,
so please come and check to see if you've been lucky.
If you are, you can take Henry home with you
tomorrow afternoon.'

The end of the lesson bell went just as Miss Temple
drew to a close. Chairs scraped on the floor, people
picked up their bags and started to file out. Miss
Temple took Justin into one corner for a stern word,
then let him go. He shuffled out. Mandy sighed
again as she noticed five or six people queuing up
to give Miss Temple their slips of paper, Vicki
Simpson and Becky Severn among them. She sidled
by, towards the door.

'How about you, Mandy?' Miss Temple asked,
knowing Mandy's love of animals. She brought her
up short.

'Sorry, Miss. I can't.'

'Going on holiday?'

Mandy shook her head. 'No. It's just that we have enough animals to take care of as it is,' she said quietly.

'Ah.' Miss Temple nodded. 'So you can't manage it?'

Mandy shrugged, but an idea shot into her head as she glanced back at Henry, still preening in the sun. 'No,' she said, her spirits suddenly lifting. 'But I think I know someone who can!'

Two

'James!' Mandy cried. The corridor was crowded with kids, all making their way outside for morning break. She'd spotted her friend's serious face with its mop of straight brown hair and round glasses. 'Wait a second!' She squeezed through the crowd towards him.

He turned and gave her a shy grin. 'Hi, Mandy.' Then he whispered to a couple of friends to go ahead without him. 'Where's the fire?' he asked, as Mandy caught up with him at last.

'No fire. But listen to this!' she gasped. Her blue eyes were sparkling. 'You know Henry?'

'Henry who?'

'Henry the Eighth.'

'Yes, sure. He was the one with six wives, wasn't he? He kept killing them off for some reason.' James's eyes twinkling behind his glasses showed that he was teasing.

'No, not *that* Henry the Eighth. *Our* Henry, the school Henry! Henry the Hamster!'

'Oh, *that* Henry.' James folded his arms. 'I might have guessed it was an animal that you'd got so worked up about.'

Mandy felt people swarm by, knocking against her with their schoolbags, barging down the corridor, heading for the sunny playground. 'I'm not worked up!' she protested. Then she grinned at James. 'OK, then, I am. But listen, I've just had this terrific idea!'

James's brown eyes widened. 'Uh-oh!'

She grabbed hold of his elbow. 'Miss Temple needs someone to take care of Henry during the school holiday,' she gabbled. 'Well, of course I'd love to do it, but I can't, as you know, because Mum and Dad have this strict rule about pets, but I thought it would be terrific if *you* could take Henry home! Wouldn't it be great if you had him? I could pop in every now and then to help you look after him. Not that you couldn't manage perfectly well by yourself, I realise, but it would be *brilliant* if we both took care of him;

if your mum and dad say yes, and if you think it's a good idea too!'

'Whoa!' James put up both hands to fend Mandy off. 'Slow down.'

Mandy had only paused for breath. 'What's the matter? Don't you want to look after Henry? He's *gorgeous*! He's really, really friendly, and he's got a very interesting personality. Hamsters need company, and I'd be able to come nearly every day to help. It's not as if you'd have to do everything . . .' Mandy began to slow down. She felt herself go hot and red. Here she was, gushing on, and James was standing calmly in the emptying corridor, arms folded, a smile spreading across his face.

'Just hang on a minute,' he said slowly.

'Why? James, you have to make your mind up pretty quickly. Miss Temple is in the lab right this minute asking for volunteers. She's going to mix the names up in a hat and draw one out. She'll have finished and gone off to the staffroom if we don't hurry up!' Mandy's enthusiasm seemed to be falling on deaf ears. 'Don't you want to put your name on the list?'

James sprang his answer on her. 'I already have!'

'What?'

'We had biology first lesson. Miss Temple asked our class the same thing. I was the first to volunteer.'

'To look after Henry?'

James nodded, watching her puzzled face.

Mandy blushed even more furiously.

'Great minds think alike,' he told her. 'When Miss Temple said that Henry needed a home for the summer, I thought, me and Mandy, quick as a flash!'

They began to walk down the steps towards the playground. 'Do you think we'll be lucky?' she wondered. 'Henry seems to be pretty popular.' She glanced up and through the window at the queue of pupils still waiting to give their names to Miss Temple.

James shrugged. 'Think positive. There's always a chance that my name will be the one!'

'OK,' she smiled. 'So you'll go straight home tonight and ask your mum and dad if it would be all right?' The sun in the sheltered playground was almost hot enough to melt the tarmac. Mandy felt the heat, and fanned her face.

James nodded. 'Do you fancy a game of tennis after tea?'

'If it's not too hot,' she agreed.

They made their arrangements to go down to the courts by the riverside. 'Do you think they'll say yes?' she asked.

'About Henry?' He nodded. 'We already have Blackie and Eric to look after. What's one little extra hamster?'

Mandy smiled. Henry wasn't just any old hamster. She suspected he would be quite a handful. But Mr and Mrs Hunter weren't to know that. And anyway, there was no point counting your chickens before they were hatched; or your hamster before your name had been drawn out of the hat, she thought.

Mandy stretched out on the patio at the back of the cottage, letting her teatime food settle before she cycled down to James's house.

In the background she could hear the sharp barks and muffled yelps of some of the residents in the unit behind the surgery. This was where the patients stayed overnight at Animal Ark, recovering from operations, or perhaps for observation, until Mr or Mrs Hope had diagnosed their ailments.

Mandy yawned. The sun had sunk lower, but the evening was still warm. She could hear her father humming to himself as he fixed up the water hose and began to sprinkle the flower-beds in their long, rambling garden.

'*Summertime . . .*' he sang, low and soulful. '*And the livin' is easy . . .*' Adam Hope put on an accent that made him sound as if he came from the American South. Mandy lay back on her lounger and grinned.

> '*Boom-boom, b-boom . . .*
> *So, hush little baby,*
> *Do-on't you-u cry-y!*'

He sprayed water over limp patches of marigolds, oomp-pahing on an imaginary saxophone. Then with a grin he swung the hose round in Mandy's direction. Cold drops rained down on her white T-shirt and hot face. She squealed and leaped to her feet.

'Da-ad!' She put her hands over her head and darted off the patio on to the grass, seeking shelter behind the apple tree.

Adam Hope, holding the hose like a fireman in an emergency, squirted water at the tree.

'Mum, help!' Mandy squealed again. She saw Emily Hope appear at the French windows, standing in her blue shorts and white sleeveless top, hands on hips, grinning at them. Mandy peered out from behind her tree. The sunlight caught in the spray, creating a million rainbow drops. 'Da-ad!' Mandy yelped again. She was soaked to the skin.

Her dad pulled at the hose once too often. It stretched and jerked, then came apart at a point where a small metal clip held two sections together. Water spurted out at Adam Hope, gushing into the air and drenching him from head to foot.

'Ha!' Mandy yelled, and staggered out on to the lawn. Her sides ached from laughing. 'Serves you right, Dad!' She watched water drip from his dark hair and beard. 'That'll teach you to leave me to sunbathe in peace!'

On the patio, Mrs Hope quietly turned off the garden tap. She popped into the kitchen for two towels and came out and thrust them at her husband and Mandy. 'Never trust your dad with a hosepipe,' she warned, her face bright in the sun. 'He just can't resist pointing it at someone. Remember when you were little, Mandy? I'd get out the paddling-pool for you in the fine weather, and before I knew it, your dad would be out here in his swimming-trunks, offering to "fill it up" for me. I'd turn my back, and there he would be, squirting everyone in sight!'

Mandy laughed. Her dad sighed. 'You're only young once!' he pointed out.

'Exactly!' Mandy raised her eyebrows at her mum. She'd finished towelling her hair and spread the towel over a branch to dry.

'Which reminds me of a conversation I had with Sam Western in the surgery earlier this afternoon,' Mr Hope said, growing more serious. He put his arm round his wife's shoulder and the three of them wandered back towards the house. 'It was to do with enjoying yourself while you're young.'

Mandy only listened with half an ear. Sam Western owned a large farm up by High Cross. He lorded it over the district and made himself unpopular with his high-handed ways, but he was a man of influence in the village. Mandy didn't care for him, because he in turn didn't care much for the animals she loved. She gathered up her tennis things as her dad chatted on about Sam Western, ready to head off to James's house.

'... Apparently Sam Western intends getting up a petition. The town council has given permission for Bert Burnley to set up a caravan park for the summer in his bottom field. A school from Birmingham wants to run activity holidays for some of their kids. But Mr Western tells me there's a lot of local opposition ... Mrs Ponsonby, Mrs Parker Smythe, the usual crew.' Mr Hope took off his wet T-shirt and wrung it out. Then he laid it to dry across the sun lounger.

Mandy gave her mum a quick kiss and told her where she was heading.

'What can they do about it if the council has already granted planning permission?' Emily Hope twisted her long red hair on to the top of her head and glanced up at the sun. She smiled and waved at Mandy. 'Don't be too late back,' she said.

'You know Sam Western. He won't take no for an answer. If *he* objects to this scheme for the caravan park by the river, then no mere town council can stand in his way. He's planning to have a sit-in or some such nonsense when the caravans arrive. And he asked me to sign his petition against the site being used as a temporary holiday centre. He says city kids will drag down the tone of the neighbourhood.'

Emily Hope frowned. 'You didn't sign?'

''Course not. I said he'd best be careful to stay on the right side of the law. If the council has said yes to the holiday centre, there's not much he can do about it.'

'What did he say?'

'He said they'd make the council pay more attention to what residents round here think.'

There was a pause as Mandy unlocked the padlock on her bike and sat astride the saddle. The conversation had began to sound interesting at the mention of kids from the city coming to stay in Welford. A summer holiday centre? A caravan site by the river? This sounded like fun. There would be lots of new faces in the village; kids her own age.

'Well,' Mrs Hope said, her face set in determined lines. '*I'm* a local resident, and *I* think it's a great idea!'

'Me too,' Mr Hope agreed. 'Don't worry, I don't suppose even Sam Western can put a stop to it.'

'When will the caravans come on to the site?'

'The day after tomorrow; Saturday, I think.'

Mandy caught his last words, freewheeling down the drive towards the lane. She headed between high hawthorn hedges towards the village.

The Hunters' house stood close to the river, at the far end of Welford. As she cycled easily towards James's house, Mandy passed by a level field full of buttercups and daisies. At the far side of the field there was a fence and beyond that a slope down to the riverbank. It was a couple of acres, and occasionally the farmer, Bert Burnley, would turn a herd of Friesian cows on to it. But generally the field was left fallow, a haven for rabbits and moles; undisturbed, lush and overgrown. This was the field for the caravans, Mandy realised.

Even now there were two men clambering out of a small red pick-up truck, one with a sledgehammer, one with a white sign attached to a post. The words on the sign were clear for Mandy to read as she cycled by. 'RIVERSIDE CARAVAN PARK' it said in big black letters. The men angled the post into the ground by the edge of the field, and, as Mandy pedalled the final fifty metres to James's house, she heard the thud of the hammer as it drove the post into the hard ground.

Good! she thought. It was proof that the summer camp would go ahead. *I wonder whether James knows he'll have a bunch of new kids staying opposite him?* She rushed inside to tell him the news.

Three

'Great!' James agreed that the caravans were a good idea. 'I've always wanted to stay in one myself.' He grabbed his racket and they set off for the courts.

They arrived to find James's mum already there, playing a gentle game in the early evening against Mrs Parker Smythe from Beacon House. The Parker Smythes were rich neighbours of Sam Western, and Mandy wasn't surprised to hear the topic of conversation as the two ladies finished their game and came off-court to rest.

'I mean to say!' Mrs Parker Smythe's narrow voice rang out above the smack of tennis rackets against balls on nearby courts. She was cool and elegant in her short white skirt, not a blonde hair out of place. Mandy easily heard every word she said. 'Who knows what sort of people we'll have coming to stay in the village? And caravans are such a glaring eyesore. Why, we might even be able to see them from our house! And these children will all come from the cities, and you can guess what they'll get up to once they're let loose on a quiet little village like Welford. Your house faces right on to the field, doesn't it?' she asked James's mum. 'You must be seething with anger!'

Mandy frowned as she trotted to the netting to retrieve two balls. Mrs Parker Smythe was being her usual snobbish self.

'Well, actually, no we're not,' Mrs Hunter said more quietly. 'We weren't keen on the idea of caravans when we first heard, it's true. But then we realised it would be just for the summer, and we thought what a lovely opportunity it was. Not just for the children who will come here on holiday, but for James and all the village children too. It's time they broadened their horizons, don't you think?' She looked Mrs Parker Smythe full in the face without toning down her opinion. As she turned away to go up the steps into the pavilion, she gave James and Mandy a small wink.

'Well!' Mrs Parker Smythe stood there stranded. She swiped at the grass with her tennis racket and looked daggers at Mandy. 'There are plenty of people round here who take the opposite view!' she announced to nobody in particular, as she flounced up the steps after Mrs Hunter.

Mandy and James played fast and furious tennis, in spite of the heat. They called it a draw at one set each, promising to take up the challenge again next time. They flopped down by the netting to take a swig of orange juice which Mandy had brought along in her bag.

'How about an ice-cream?' James suggested.

Mandy nodded and they were soon on their bikes cycling back towards the village, past the newly erected sign.

'I'm glad your mum put Mrs Parker Smythe in her place,' Mandy said, glancing at the empty field. But she knew that Mr Western and Mrs Parker Smythe were not the sort to give in easily. She wasn't surprised to see a small knot of people gathered together up ahead, standing round the low silver car belonging to Mrs Parker Smythe which was parked just outside the post office in the centre of the village. She could hear arguments flying back and forth. Feelings were running high.

'I think it's an absolute disgrace!' Mrs Ponsonby proclaimed. Her Pekinese dog, Pandora, sat growling at her feet. 'The whole village will be swamped by strangers, and these city children aren't brought up to follow the country code! They'll leave gates open and sheep will wander on to the roads. They won't keep to public footpaths as they ought, and they will climb walls, you mark my words!' Somehow, the fusspot of Welford managed to make it sound like a hanging offence. 'And goodness knows what else they'll get up to!' she said darkly.

Mandy got off her bike and passed by the group, pausing to stroke Pandora and Mrs Ponsonby's lovable mongrel, Toby. Ernie Bell sat on the bench outside the post office, listening quietly. He shook his head. 'I reckon we should hold our horses before we all go overboard,' he warned. 'We musn't give a dog a bad name, you know.'

A strange, muddled picture of horses, ships and dogs jumbled in Mandy's mind, but she agreed with Ernie; the visitors should be given a fair chance.

She followed James into the cool, shaded interiors of the McFarlanes' shop to buy their ice-cream. When they came out, Mrs Parker Smythe was still gathering support for the anti-caravan campaign.

'Our first aim must be to stop them moving on to the site in the first place,' she ordered. 'It's all very well for Mr Burnley to wave his planning permission all over the place, but he's flying in the face of important local opinion.'

Mrs Ponsonby nodded. Toby, bored with the proceedings, trotted up to Mandy and sat with his tongue out, gazing longingly at her ice-cream.

'The first caravans are due to arrive on Saturday morning,' Mrs Parker Smythe went on. 'Our plan is to block their way in the lane. Mr Western will get his workers to drive tractors down and park across the gateway to the field. We must all be there to lend support!'

Ernie cleared his throat. 'And risk being carted off to the police station in Walton?' he said to the small crowd. 'It's against the law to obstruct a public highway, remember!'

Mandy and James agreed. She was concentrating so hard on the argument that her ice-cream cone tipped sideways, and the half-melted contents slipped out. But it had no chance to hit the ground; Toby caught it like a cricketer diving for a catch in the slips. He gobbled it in one gulp. Mandy's mouth dropped open in surprise.

'Shh!' James warned. If Mrs Ponsonby found out

she'd be rushing poor Toby straight over to Animal Ark with a near-fatal case of *frozen stomachitis*! Meanwhile, Pandora shuffled across to stare up at James's ice-cream.

'We must be prepared to stand by our principles!' Mrs Ponsonby took up the argument against the new caravans. 'We must make it clear that Welford is against changes of this sort, made without a by-your-leave.' She jutted out her double chin and pulled back her shoulders like a soldier on parade. The frills down the front of her powder-blue frock shook with outrage.

James slipped Pandora the remains of his ice-cream, cornet and all. He'd been won over by the Pekinese's huge, dark eyes. The ice-cream disappeared in a flash.

'Toby, Pandora, come here!' Mrs Ponsonby clapped her plump hands for their attention. 'Come here, good doggies!'

They both yawned and ignored her.

'Go on, Pandora. Go on, Toby!' Mandy whispered.

Reluctantly they obeyed her and trotted towards their owner.

Mrs Parker Smythe had started up the smooth engine of her silver car, and Mrs Ponsonby began to make her way up the street, head held high. People began to disperse, grumbling and muttering about the new caravan site.

Mandy looked at Ernie scratching his stubbly grey head. He gazed back at James and Mandy. 'Some folk round here don't have enough to do to keep them out of mischief,' he complained. 'And you know what they say; the devil makes work for idle hands.'

Soon the street was empty. As the sun began to sink, a golden red glow seeped into the sky. Mandy said goodbye to James, ready to head for home. 'Let's keep our fingers crossed,' she said, her mind flying back for a moment to the really important and interesting things in life: animals, and, more specifically, their hopes of looking after Henry.

'We'll find out tomorrow morning,' he reminded her.

'Let's go into school ten minutes early,' she suggested. 'To see if Miss Temple's picked out the name.'

They arranged to meet outside the post office at eight o'clock, then they rode off on their separate ways. James waved at Ernie and passed on by the new sign for the caravan site. Then he turned right, up his drive. Mandy rode up her lane towards the sunset, taking James's advice and thinking positive thoughts. 'We *will* be lucky,' she said over and over. 'We *will* be lucky and get to look after Henry for the summer!'

They gathered outside the biology lab before morning registration; Mandy and James, Vicki Simpson and her friend, Becky Severn, and Brandon Gill who lived at Greystones Farm. Altogether, Mandy counted twenty-three hopefuls, all waiting to see who would look after the school hamster.

She peered through the window into the empty lab. In one corner she spotted Henry's cage; a roomy, hardwood box with a removable glass front and a wire-mesh lid. Inside the box was a day area covered in fresh hay, with a drinking bowl in one corner. And there was a small 'upstairs' compartment; a box within a box, which Henry could enter via a sloping ramp. He used this private bedroom for his frequent daytime naps. And of course, in one corner was the exercise wheel.

Mandy could see him now, trundling away. He reminded her of a stout man jogging for his health, determined to get his daily exercise. She nudged James and pointed to the cage. 'Look at him,' she smiled.

'It will do him good,' he assured her. 'Did you

know, they found out that some hamsters run eight kilometres a night on those exercise wheels?'

Mandy let this sink in. 'Eight kilometres? Then why is he so fat?'

'I didn't say that *Henry* runs eight kilometres,' James pointed out. 'He probably just comes out to use the wheel when he knows someone's looking, to show off. I bet Henry just snacks and snoozes the night away!'

'Are you saying he's lazy?' Mandy pretended she wouldn't hear a word said against the hamster. 'If you ask me, it's not his fault he's so fat.'

'Whose is it, then?'

'It's all those people's who feed him crisps from their lunch boxes, obviously! You can't blame a poor little hamster for eating all the wrong, fattening foods, can you?'

'Hmm.' James looked thoughtful. 'I suppose not.'

Mandy nodded and looked up the corridor. 'Hurry up, Miss Temple!' she pleaded. She noticed Vicki Simpson whispering behind her hand to Becky. She ignored this and smiled at Brandon. 'How's Ruby?' she asked. Ruby was Brandon's pet pig.

'Grand,' Brandon said in his broad, no-nonsense way. 'We're going over to Walton this weekend to show her. We reckon we're in with a chance of a prize.'

Mandy was wishing him luck when Miss Temple appeared at the end of the corridor. She walked briskly towards them. Everyone fell silent. All eyes were on the young teacher as she unlocked the lab and invited them in.

'Sit down for a moment.' She put down her bag and turned towards them. 'Now, I haven't made the draw yet. I wanted you all to see that it's fair and above board.' She picked up a cardboard box. 'Since I haven't got a hat, this will have to do. All the names are in here on folded pieces of paper.'

Mandy fixed her eyes on the box. 'We *will* be

lucky!' she repeated silently to herself.

Miss Temple smiled at them all. 'We only have a few moments before the bell goes for registration,' she said. 'So who wants to pick the name out of the box?'

A forest of hands shot up.

'Becky, you're nearest. You come and do it for us.' Miss Temple held the box up above eye level so Becky couldn't see which paper she chose. 'Just reach up and draw one out. That's it.'

Becky stood on tiptoe. Mandy held her breath and kept her fingers crossed. She watched as Becky took a piece of paper from the box and handed it to Miss Temple. The teacher unfolded it and laid it flat on the bench. She looked along the rows. 'James Hunter,' she announced, clear as a bell.

James gasped. Mandy couldn't believe her ears. Several of the others smiled wistfully and shuffled off. Miss Temple held open the door and said sorry to the unlucky ones. But Becky frowned and muttered to Vicki, ' . . . Seems a bit suspicious to me . . . can't be coincidence . . . Mandy is teacher's pet, we all know that . . . and James Hunter is her best friend!'

Vicki nodded. 'It was probably all a big fix.'

Miss Temple, busy now telling James where to find

her after school, overheard them. She turned to speak. 'Vicki, Becky, I'm sorry you're disappointed,' she said quietly. 'But so are about twenty other people. I can't let you go around school all day with those long faces. You just have to accept the luck of the draw.' She waited patiently until the two girls returned her gaze. 'That's better. And don't let me hear that you've been spreading false rumours that this was all done out of favouritism. It was nothing of the kind, as you very well know.'

Vicki and Becky blushed. 'Yes, Miss. Sorry, Miss,' they said.

'Well, go off to registration, and we'll hear no more about a fix. You too, Mandy and James, or else you'll all be in trouble for being late.'

They nodded and hurried down the corridor, hard on the heels of the two disgruntled girls. Only now could Mandy begin to believe their luck. She gave a little skip and a jump.

'What did I tell you about the power of positive thinking?' James grinned. They took the stairs two at a time.

'Pure luck!' Mandy teased.

'Says you!' Before he split off down a separate corridor, he paused. 'You know Henry's weight problem?' he reminded her.

She caught his eye. 'Can I guess what you're thinking?'

'I'm thinking fresh vegetables, dried oats, nuts and rusks!'

'No more crisps?' She began to smile. 'James, you're planning to put Henry on a diet!'

'A calorie count,' he confirmed.

'A strict regime.'

'An exercise plan, so we can bring him back in September looking like a new hamster. No more excess fat.' He grinned.

'Poor Henry.' Mandy shook her head. 'I suppose it's for his own good, though.'

'Poor Henry, nothing! My house is going to be the first hamster health farm in the country. What do you think, Mandy?'

She pondered the challenge. 'You're right,' she decided. 'No biscuits, no cakes!'

'Good. See you at four in the lab?' he asked. They would take Henry home together.

'You bet!' She sped off to her own classroom. They had Henry to themselves for the whole summer. They'd give him the best of everything, and make him stick to his healthy diet. They might even be able to take him on outings, down to the river for a picnic in the fresh air. Mandy made great plans. She sat at her desk just as her form teacher, Mr Meldrum, arrived. Her head was in the clouds, doting on Henry, when he called her name from the register.

'Mandy Hope?' he repeated sharply.

'Yes, Mr Meldrum!' she called. Four o'clock couldn't come soon enough. Then the whole summer holiday was spread before them; endless days of looking after Henry!

Four

It was early Saturday morning. Mandy had been up for ages, busy doing chores at Animal Ark before Simon, their nurse, had even arrived. She cleaned out cages and talked to the parrot, the gerbil and the black Labrador who'd been kept overnight in the unit. She knew that good hygiene was a top priority for a vet, and anyway, she loved the company of animals, talking to them and encouraging them to get back on their feet after an illness.

Simon came in promptly at half-past eight to find everywhere spotless and ready for surgery. He chatted with Mandy for a few minutes while Jean Knox, the receptionist, prepared the appointment list. 'What's it feel like to have six whole weeks of freedom?' he asked.

'Brilliant!' Mandy bubbled with enthusiasm. She took off her white coat and hung it on a peg in one of the treatment rooms. 'James has brought home the school hamster for the holiday. We're going to take him down to the river for a picnic.'

'Lucky hamster,' Simon said with a grin. He was young and easy-going. 'I had a hamster when I was a kid. She was called Honey; a light golden one with beautiful ruby eyes. But she couldn't see a metre in front of her nose. Hamsters can't, you know. They're very short-sighted.'

Mandy nodded and made a mental note.

'They use their whiskers to feel their way about. They're nocturnal; dozy by day and active by night.'

Again Mandy nodded. 'Henry won't come to any harm if we take him on outings, will he?'

Simon smiled. 'He'll think he's in seventh heaven. I take it he's tame?'

'Very. He likes to be out of his cage. He sits in your hand and loves being stroked. And fed! That's his problem, actually.'

Simon smiled. 'Just watch what you give him to eat, that's all. No chocolate for a start. It's poisonous for hamsters. Apples are fine. Sunflower seeds are

their favourite, and full of protein. They love biscuits
and cake as well, but not too often.'

Mandy's face lit up. 'We plan to put him on a diet;
fruit and greens, nuts and cereals. No sugar. We
want him to lose weight.'

'Very good.' Simon followed her into reception
and smiled at Jean, fixing his glasses firmly on his
nose. 'Does Henry know about this slimming
regime?'

'Not yet.' Mandy had reached the door, eager to
be on her way down to James's house.

'Best of luck,' he called. 'And remember, be strict
with Henry. Don't let him get round you with those
big soft eyes. I know you!' He laughed as he watched
her swing her leg over her bicycle saddle.

'Could you tell Mum I won't be back for lunch?'
Mandy called before she sped off. 'Mrs Hunter's
making us a packed lunch and we're taking Henry
out for his treat!' She whizzed down the lane. The
sun was still shining, the trees rustled in a slight
breeze; a perfect day for a picnic.

Mandy lay flat on her back. The nearby river rippled
and swirled, the sand was warm in the sun.

'Pass me another lettuce leaf for Henry,' James
murmured. He sat cross-legged on the pebbles, with

the hamster nestled in the palm of his hand. Henry was lazily grooming behind his ears with his tiny front paws. His cage was set carefully to one side.

Mandy reached out an arm and felt for the hamper which James's mum had packed. Her fingers made contact with the wickerwork top. She flipped it open and rummaged inside without raising her head to look. Sun, sandwiches and lemonade had made her sleepy.

James got up, balancing Henry in his hand. 'Don't worry, I'll do it. Anyway, why are you in such a lazy mood?'

'I'll have you know I was up at the crack of dawn!' she sighed. She opened one eye as James crouched beside the hamper. Henry's nose and whiskers twitched with interest.

'James, watch out!' Mandy sat bolt upright, but her cry came too late. Henry had launched himself from the palm of James's hand, straight into the hamper. He landed with a thud amongst the leftover biscuits. Real food! Beautiful calories! He tucked in happily.

James panicked. He hadn't seen where Henry had landed. 'Where is he? Quick, Mandy, where's he gone?' He scrambled a few metres up the bank into some long grass. 'Henry's escaped. Help me look!'

Mandy gazed down at a happy hamster. 'He's in here,' she said calmly. 'In the hamper.' She knelt for a closer look. 'Oh, Henry!' she scolded. She heard James creep up behind her. Together they peered into the shadowy safety of the picnic basket. Henry was nibbling biscuits to his heart's content. He munched and stored the crumbs in his cheeks, shoving biscuit into his mouth as fast as he could. Mandy glanced at James.

'Henry, the calories!' James stood his head.

'A fat lot he cares!' Mandy began to smile. 'And it's no good offering him lettuce now, not when there's a heap of broken biscuits to get at!'

Henry cocked his head at them. His bright eyes twinkled, his cheeks pouched out to twice their normal size.

'Come here, Henry.' James reached into the hamper and cupped both hands under Henry's fat little belly. He tried to sound severe, but a grin was spreading over his face too. 'So much for getting you slim! Oh, well, it could have been worse.'

'How come?'

'He could have actually made a run for it, I suppose. It would have taken us all afternoon to find him in that long grass. Thank heavens he landed in the hamper.'

Mandy shook her head. 'Henry knows which side his bread is buttered,' she said. Then she giggled.

'Or which way the cookie crumbles!' James laughed. 'But it's ruined his diet. We'll have to make him have an extra go on his wheel tonight, and nothing but lettuce for him tomorrow!'

Henry twitched his nose.

'I don't think he likes that idea.' Mandy watched James carry the hamster back to his cage. 'Time to be getting back,' she said. She tidied the hamper and closed its lid. 'I promised Dad I'd lend a hand with afternoon surgery.'

Henry's little escapade had brought them back to earth. It was all very well drifting through the sunny day on the riverbank like this, but there were jobs to do. She sighed as she stood up and straightened her T-shirt. 'Hey,' she said, glancing beyond the river into the field beyond. 'What's going on over there?'

There was a cluster of cars gathering on the narrow road. Two tractors came trundling down the lane after them, and a group of people stood by the gate into the field, talking loudly.

'It's that lot protesting about the caravans,' James said. He picked up the hamster cage and climbed on to the path. 'Mrs Ponsonby and the rest.'

Mandy spied a wide-brimmed pink hat in the

middle of the small crowd. And then she recognised Mrs Parker Smythe's low, silver car. In the distance, she saw a huge lorry with a trailer carrying the first of the caravans. It crawled slowly towards the recently formed roadblock. Voices rose. Someone brought out a placard and raised it in the air.

'Come on!' Mandy said, picking up the hamper. 'Let's cut across and see what's going on!'

By the time they reached the gate, the protest was well underway. A second lorry with its enormous load had pulled up behind the first. James spotted a police car bringing up the rear and pointed it out to Mandy. 'Police escort,' he whispered. 'This could be serious!'

But Mandy couldn't help smiling at the gang of activists. They were an odd bunch to be breaking the law. Mrs Parker Smythe, more at home at a cocktail party, tried to look the part of a protester in a pair of well-cut black trousers and a crisp white shirt. But Mrs Ponsonby looked as if she was dressed for a garden party in her flower-laden hat and tight-fitting frock. Her stout face was red with the effort of protest, as she waved her cardboard placard high in the air. 'No Welcome to Caravanners in Welford!' it said on one side, 'Welford Says No to the Caravans!' on the other.

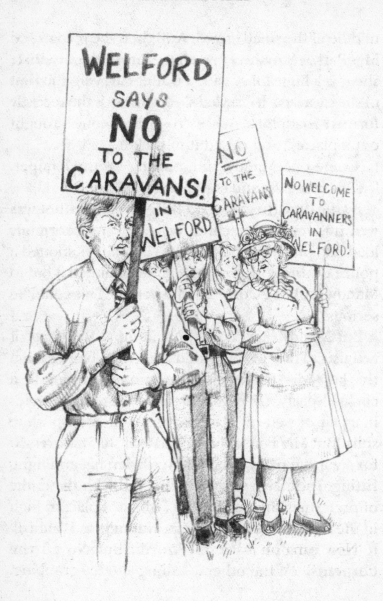

The two women took their orders, along with five or six other protesters, from the sturdy figure of Mr Western, who stood and directed operations like an army major. 'Watch your right flank!' he warned as Bert Burnley, the farmer who'd agreed to have the caravans on his land, came down the hill from his farm.

His Land-rover soon drew to a halt and he jumped out and strode across. He seized hold of the gate and let it off the latch. It swung free. Obligingly Mandy stood just inside the entrance to the field, holding it wide open.

'What's all the rumpus?' Mr Burnley growled. He was a thickset man with a wide, ruddy face and crinkly grey hair. 'Don't you know I've had council permission for this since Easter? Why not pack up and go home, or I'll get the police to act!' He glared at Sam Western, who strode towards him, hands on hips.

'Why don't you listen to what people have to say before you rush ahead with your money-grabbing scheme?' Mr Western shouted, centimetres from the burly farmer's angry face.

'Hear, hear!' Mrs Ponsonby chimed in.

'Now hang on just a minute.' Mr Burnley's frown deepened. 'Who are you calling money-grabbing,

Western? You'd best check your facts before you start
accusing people!'

Mandy kept one eye on the arguing men, one eye
on the approaching policeman. Behind the blue-
uniformed figure she caught sight of a young,
fair-haired reporter from the local paper, camera at
the ready. She pointed him out to James. 'The
newspaper's in on the act!' The row could develop
into a local headline.

Mr Western snorted. His supporters rallied round,
as the policeman, the reporter and two lorry drivers
skirted around Western's tractors that were blocking
the road.

'I said, check your facts,' Burnley roared. 'And
you'll find I'm letting the caravans use this field rent-
free. It's for a good cause, and I've told Kingsmill
School to go ahead and give the kids a proper
holiday, free of charge. It's time someone round here
did something for nothing!' He squared up to Mr
Western, red in the face. Mrs Ponsonby, Mrs Parker
Smythe and the others looked taken aback.

'Hear, hear!' Mandy and James cried.

Mr Western blustered. 'Well, whether or not you're
lining your own pockets, Bert Burnley, we still don't
want the eyesore of a whole lot of caravans spoiling
the look of the place. And we wont budge from here

until you tell those lorry drivers to back off down that lane and take those trailers back where they came from!'

He didn't see the tall figure of the policeman loom up behind him, but Mandy and James did. They saw the reporter raise his camera and start to take shots of the protesters and their placards. They heard them fall quiet in the full glare of publicity. One or two crept away to their cars before they could be photographed.

'This will be in the paper on Monday,' someone whispered. 'I never bargained for that.' He went and sat quietly in his car, looking as if he wished the ground would swallow him.

But Mrs Ponsonby stood firm. She glared at the young policeman as he approached Sam Western and ordered him to tell his lads to move their tractors. 'Welford Says No!' she chanted.

The journalist wrote notes: Mr Western argued their case.

It was all to no avail. The policeman sternly pointed out that what they were doing was against the law. Mandy and James stood alongside Mr Burnley, happy to be photographed. 'We think it's a great idea,' Mandy told the reporter. 'Everyone should be able to come and enjoy the countryside.

We're looking forward to meeting these new kids. And I'd just like to say that not many people in Welford are against the idea of the caravan park. I think you should put that in your article!'

Mrs Parker Smythe overheard and tossed her head. Mrs Ponsonby glowered. But Mandy and James stood, one to either side of Mr Burnley, proudly facing the camera, under the bright new sign for Riverside Caravan Park.

'Thanks. It should make the front page on Monday,' the reporter told them.

'By the way, did you get Henry in the photograph?' Mandy asked. They watched as the policeman cleared off the protesters. Gradually the sit-in fell apart. Mrs Ponsonby stopped chanting and lowered her placard, Mr Western at last gave an order for the tractors to back off.

'Who's Henry?' The journalist packed away his notebook and camera, ready to dash off to file his report.

'The hamster.' Mandy pointed to the cage, where Henry stared contentedly at proceedings, his cheeks still pleasantly full of biscuit.

'Oh, yes; the hamster's in the shot, don't you worry,' the reporter said with a smile.

And so the protest faded. The protesters went

home, red-faced and grumbling, unused to losing an argument. Then the lorries trundled into the field with their huge caravans, while Mr Burnley shook hands with a young man and woman; two teachers from Kingsmill School who were organising the holiday centre.

'Thanks very much,' the young man said to Mandy, when he heard from the farmer the part Mandy and James had played.

Mandy blushed. 'We were glad to help.'

She and James said hello to the young woman, Chrissie Searle. The man was called Pete Cavendish. Both leaders were young and pleasant looking outdoor types in shorts and T-shirts. But they were too busy to stop and talk for long. 'The first batch of kids is due to arrive on Monday,' Pete Cavendish said. 'And there's loads to do before then.'

Satisfied, they went off their separate ways. Full of the latest news, James and Mandy went back to his house with Henry. Then Mandy hurried on home, passed the wooden sign with 'Animal Ark, Veterinary Surgeon' carved on it, and into the house to tell her mum and dad she'd be in the newspaper. The protest had collapsed, the caravans were moving in, and Mr Western had admitted defeat.

Emily Hope smiled and gave her a hug. 'That's

my girl!' she said after she'd listened to what Mandy had said to the reporter. 'I couldn't have put it better myself!'

Five

There was no doubt about it, Sam Western and his followers had made fools of themselves. Everyone at Animal Ark agreed that their picture on the front page of the newspaper on Monday morning made them out to be small-minded snobs. Mandy's own quote made the headline: 'A GREAT IDEA!' she read in bold, black capitals. Underneath the one of the protesters there was another good, clear picture of James holding Henry's cage, standing alongside Mr Burnley and Mandy, with a caption which read, 'Supporters of the caravan site.'

Mandy beamed across the breakfast table at her gran and grandad. They'd dropped in to show her the newspaper on their way back home from the village. Lilac Cottage, their pretty house, was down the lane from Animal Ark.

'So when do we expect the first arrivals?' Grandad asked.

'This morning. Pete and Chrissie have had to work like mad to get things ready. There are six caravans on the site, and a big Portakabin in the middle of the field, for a shop and clubhouse combined. They've got things really well organised now.'

'Pete and Chrissie?' Gran interrupted.

'Pete Cavendish and Chrissie Searle. They're the teachers from Kingsmill School in Birmingham.'

'And you're on first name terms already?' Gran teased.

'Yes. I think they're great. They plan to take the kids canoeing and mountain biking for a start, and if the weather stays fine, there's going to be a barbecue by the river at the end of the week!' Mandy was up on her feet, gulping down the last of her orange juice. 'Sorry, Gran, sorry, Grandad; I have to dash. I promised James I'd meet up with him in the village. We want to go and say hello to the first group when they arrive. Chrissie said she thought it would help to make them feel more at home. They're bound to find things pretty strange here in Welford if they come from a big city like Birmingham!'

She gave her grandparents a quick kiss and was on her way, grabbing her bike and whizzing down the lane.

James, ready and waiting in the yard outside the Fox and Goose, waved a greeting. 'I saw the Kingsmill mini-bus turn down our road five minutes ago,' he told her. They pedalled together down the main street.

Mandy nodded. 'How's Henry?'

'Great. He's back on his diet again; sunflower seeds and slices of apple. I left his cage in the fresh air on the front porch. Mum says she'll keep an eye on him.'

They cycled easily and quickly along the flat stretch of road. Up ahead, over the tops of the hawthorn hedges, they could see the gleaming new caravans in Mr Burnley's field.

'OK?' Mandy asked. They propped their bikes against the gatepost and went into the field.

She felt suddenly shy as she stepped through the long grass towards the grey Portakabin. But she thought how much more strange things must seem to the newcomers who sat on the grass outside the hut, looking warily at her and James as they approached.

'Hi,' she said to a sea of faces; a dozen or so kids of about her own age, some propped back on their elbows, some lounging against the wall of the hut, some pretending not to notice her and James. Mandy saw one girl standing apart from the rest. She was small and skinny, with wild red hair and grey-green eyes. 'I'm Mandy Hope,' she said. 'I live here in Welford.'

The girl stared shyly back. She nodded, but didn't open her mouth to speak.

'Never mind her,' one boy said. 'You can't get a word out of her. Anyone fancy a game of footie?' He picked up a white plastic ball and rolled it into the space in front of the hut.

Several voices chorused 'Yes.' James nodded, glad to join in. Soon the ball was being booted up and down the field to the sound of excited yells, calls of foul and claims for penalty kicks.

Mandy grinned at the shy girl. 'Who's the boy with the football?' she asked. He dribbled the ball expertly and passed it, shouting out instructions.

'Paul.' The answer came out almost a whisper.

'And who's the girl with the blonde hair?'

'Sonia.'

Mandy tried her best to commit their names to memory. 'Who are you?'

'Leanne Jackson.' The girl delivered her own name with a blush that coloured the whole of her face. 'I'm new at Kingsmill.'

'Are you all from the same school?'

'Yes, but I've only been there since May. My mum and me had to move house. That's why I changed schools again.'

Mandy went carefully ahead. She glanced at Leanne, then back at the football game. 'My mum's got the same colour hair as you. Only, she's not my actual mum. My real mum and dad died in an accident just after I was born. I'm adopted.'

Leanne raised her eyes from the buttercups at her feet and stared at Mandy. 'Have you got a dad?'

Mandy nodded. 'He's the local vet. So's my mum. He's lived in Welford all his life.'

A sigh escaped from Leanne. 'A vet? Have you got loads and loads of animals at your house?'

'Sort of. Only, they're not mine; they're patients at the surgery. Dogs, cats, rabbits, donkeys, ponies; you name it. Oh, and I do have three pet rabbits of my own.'

Leanne sighed again. 'Lucky thing.'

'Don't you have any pets?' Mandy was happy to chat on about her favourite subject. The two of them sat down cross-legged on the grass, one eye on the noisy game. Sonia, in goal, saved one of Paul's shots. A fresh cheer went up.

'No, I'm not allowed,' Leanne said. 'My mum and me live in a flat, and we can't keep pets.'

Mandy said she thought it was a shame. Behind her shyness, Leanne seemed friendly and easy to talk to.

'I'd love to have one,' she went on wistfully. 'A pet all of my own to look after, I mean. I've always wanted to. But we move around too much. My mum says it wouldn't be fair on any animal.'

'I suppose so.' Mandy thought for a second. 'Listen, Leanne, why don't we go over to James's house? I'm sure he won't mind, and there's something I'd like to show you. He lives just across the road; it won't take long!'

Slowly, awkwardly, Leanne got to her feet. 'OK.'

'Great!' Mandy led the way out of the field, across the narrow road. They jogged past Claire MacKay's house, where the sign for 'Rosa's Refuge' hung from a tree in the garden. 'Claire looks after hedgehogs,' Mandy explained. 'She's quite new to the village, but she soon settled in once she'd set up the refuge.' She smiled at Leanne as they went through James's gate and up the garden path.

James's Labrador must have heard their footsteps,

for he came bounding down the side of the house, tail wagging. Mandy gave him a hug. 'This is Blackie,' she said to Leanne. 'And the little cat asleep on the mat is Eric.'

Leanne went up the step and bent to stroke his soft, warm head. Eric purred. 'He's lovely,' she sighed.

Mandy pointed to the wooden cage on a shelf in the front porch. 'And this is Henry.'

'A hamster!' Leanne's eyes lit up. 'Oh, he's gorgeous!'

Henry, aware of his admiring audience, responded by jumping into the exercise wheel. He set it in motion with his feet, easily keeping his balance as he trundled away.

'He's a golden hamster. He's six months old. He belongs to our school, but James is looking after him for the holiday,' Mandy explained, glad to see Leanne's face beaming down at Henry. 'Do you know much about hamsters? They're desert rodents. They're hoarders.' She reeled off the facts.

'I know. Born in a litter of six to ten infants, without hair. Eyes open on the twelfth day. Life span two to three years.'

'Hey!' Mandy was impressed.

'I've read all about them in my pets book. But I've

never actually been this close to one before.' She gazed into the cage as Henry clambered out of the wheel and came up to the front of the cage, whiskers twitching.

'Would you like to hold him?'

Leanne nodded. She held her breath as Mandy cupped her hands under Henry, lifted him out of the cage and gave him to her. Henry nibbled her finger, then nestled contentedly in her palm. 'Oh!' she said, speechless.

'I expect you'll be able to come and see Henry whenever you like,' Mandy promised. 'James won't mind. And I come down here most days, to help look after him. Staying at Riverside means you're really close at hand.'

With her free hand Leanne stroked Henry's golden coat. 'He's so soft! His feet tickle!'

'Try giving him this.' Mandy handed her a slice of apple from a plastic bag on the shelf. She watched as the hamster took it and began to nibble. They both smiled.

At last, Leanne reached forward to put Henry back in his cage. 'I'd better be going.' The smile had begun to fade.

'But you'll come again?'

'Yes, please.'

Mandy fastened the lock. Leanne took a last look at Henry, then stroked Eric as Mandy went to play in the garden with Blackie. Just then, Mrs Hunter stuck her head through the kitchen window and waved. 'Hello, Mandy!'

'Hi, Mrs Hunter. This is Leanne Jackson from Birmingham.'

'Hello, Leanne. Nice to meet you. I hope you have a good time here in Welford.' Mrs Hunter smiled and turned back to Mandy. 'Can you tell James to come home for lunch at twelve-thirty?'

Mandy promised: then she and her new friend headed back for the caravan field. By the time they got there, the football game was coming to an end, with a three-two victory for Paul's team. Leanne nodded quietly at Mandy and slipped away to her caravan before the crowd of thirsty players charged up to the shop for cans of Coke.

James, already part of the gang, introduced Mandy to Ben, a tall boy with bristly hair. Ben was a joker, and obviously fashion-mad. He wore all the latest sports gear, pleased to have the others looking up to him. Mandy smiled and settled in with the crowd, soon forgetting about lonely Leanne.

'What shall we do now?' Sonia demanded with a yawn. She came out of the shop and flopped to the ground. 'Not much going on round here, is there?'

Her friend, Marcie, sprinkled a handful of daisy petals in her hair. 'Stop moaning, Sonia.' Marcie's broad face was cheerful and friendly. She grinned up at Mandy. 'She never stops complaining, that's her problem.'

'Yes I do. The country's boring, that's all!' Sonia stared at the hillside. 'Nothing happens. No shops, no coffee bars. I don't know why I said I'd come!'

'See!' Marcie laughed.

'Aagh, what was that?' Sonia squirmed and tried to wriggle one arm up the back of her T-shirt. 'Something's alive in there! Ouch! Get it out, Marcie!' She sprang up, yelping and dancing around in panic.

'Stand still then!' Marcie giggled. She fished about and pulled a flattened daisy from under her friend's shirt. 'Very alive, I'm sure!'

Sonia scowled and flounced off to her caravan. 'Well! Anyway, I hate the countryside!' she wailed.

Mandy turned to Ben, who was trying to persuade a red-eyed boy called Sean to go swimming in the river. 'James says it's not that deep. And I bet it's dead warm! Come on, what are we waiting for?'

'I dunno.' Sean frowned. 'I think I'm allergic to something round here.' His light brown hair flopped over his forehead, his brown eyes streamed.

'Hay fever?' Mandy suggested.

Sean groaned. 'Call this a holiday? Just stick me down on a beach somewhere hot like Spain or Greece, will you? I can't stand all these flowers!'

'There's a beach by the river,' James suggested. 'And if you stay by the water, your hay fever won't be so bad.' He ran ahead, followed by Ben and a reluctant Sean.

Mandy watched the field empty, as all the Kingsmill kids went off in different directions. They were a mixed bunch, and they hadn't all settled in yet, but she'd taken to Leanne from the start. She hoped to see her again soon. Waving at Chrissie Searle inside the shop, Mandy went to get her bike and rode slowly back to Animal Ark.

By early Wednesday morning, Mandy found that the freedom to come and go as she pleased had really sunk in. She loved the feeling of not being tied to school routine. It meant she was able to help out more at the surgery, and to ride her bike around the village, or to visit friends up on farms.

But there was already gossip in the village about the children at Riverside. There was tittle-tattle in McFarlane's when Mandy popped in for postage stamps for her gran. Mrs Ponsonby was in the thick of it, of course, advising Susan Price not to get mixed up with the newcomers. 'They're a thoroughly bad lot,' she warned. 'I'm sure your parents wouldn't want you to mix with them, Susan dear.'

Susan was in her riding gear. She made a secret grimace at Mandy. 'Thanks, Mrs Ponsonby,' she said breezily. 'Anyway, I'm riding Prince in the gymkhana over at Kenley next week, so I've got a lot of work on my hands to get him up to scratch.'

'Quite right; keep you out of mischief.' As the shop bell rang and Susan made her escape down the steps, Mrs Ponsonby turned to Mr McFarlane to report the latest wrongdoings of the city children. 'They've been here less than three days, and already they've caused havoc in the village! They have left gates open, of course, and it had to be on poor Mr Western's land, just as I said, and Dennis Saville had to round up several cows from the moor road. It's a wonder none of the poor beasts was injured!'

'Are they sure it was the children from Riverside, Mrs Ponsonby?' Mr McFarlane slowly weighed out a hundred grammes of mint toffees.

'Of course. Mr Western saw them with his own eyes. And the noise from the site is dreadful. Loud music until late at night. Wild games. Shrieking and shouting and playing in the river. I shouldn't be

surprised if someone were to drown!' Mrs Ponsonby
took off her pink-framed glasses and wiped them
on a tiny lace handkerchief. She fixed them primly
back on her nose, then turned to Mandy. 'You can't
say I didn't warn you!' she said in triumph.

Mandy bit her tongue. 'Five first class stamps
please,' she said to the shopkeeper, as Mrs Ponsonby
took her bag of sweets and sailed out of the shop.

She must have been scowling because Mr
McFarlane winked and said, 'Take no notice.'

'That's all very well, but other people might believe
what she says,' Mandy grumbled. She didn't want
Mrs Ponsonby to spoil things for the Riverside
crowd. So far, they had enjoyed their mountain
biking and canoeing activities, and there had been
no major incident, but Mrs Ponsonby and Mrs Parker
Smythe kept their eagle eyes constantly open, and
Mr Western was poised to send off his petition to
the council at the first sign of real trouble. Mandy
paid her money for the stamps and made her way
out with a shake of her head.

But she was stopped in her tracks by a scene in
the heart of the village. A group, including Ernie
Bell and his friend, Walter Pickard, with Betty Hilder
from the animal sanctuary and Mandy's friend John
Hardy from the pub, had gathered by Walter's

garden wall. In their midst, Mrs Ponsonby stood examining fresh evidence.

'You say they were standing on your wall-top?' she asked in a loud voice.

They stared at something lying at their feet. With a sinking heart, Mandy got off her bike and went to take a look.

'Same as always,' Walter agreed. 'It's a nice sunny position, see.'

Peering over the wall, in amongst the feet of the bystanders, Mandy could see the remains of clay flowerpots, scattered earth, and half a dozen uprooted geranium plants. They were all trampled into the flagstones in Walter's yard. She glanced up at the old man's dismayed face. She knew he tended his plants with care. The geraniums brightened up the row of little stone cottages year after year, and Walter could hardly afford to replace them at this time. Whoever had done this must have been acting out of mischief, not knowing how much the flowers meant to him.

'Did you see who did it?' Ernie asked, his voice tense with annoyance.

Walter shook his head. 'I just opened the door to collect my milk from the step and there they were, all smashed!'

'It's obvious,' Mrs Ponsonby told them. 'Didn't I tell you that those children from the caravan site were running wild? I knew there's be some serious damage before too long!' She fixed them with her beady eyes.

'But you can't be sure,' Betty Hilder objected. 'Not if Walter didn't actually see them do it.'

'It stands to reason. We never had a moment's trouble in the village before those young hooligans came along. Now every day there's something new. Cattle on the loose. Loud late-night parties. And now vandalism!' Mrs Ponsonby let this last word roll richly round her tongue.

'Hmm.' Walter shook his head. 'Whoever it is, it

won't stick them pots back together, and it won't revive them poor geraniums neither.'

'But I did try to warn you all,' Mrs Ponsonby insisted. 'I knew that the caravan site spelt trouble, only none of you would listen.' She sniffed and glared at Mandy. 'Well, I hope you're satisfied!' she said, stalking off down the street.

Shaken, Mandy couldn't find the nerve to defend the city children in front of poor Walter. Betty ran to the pub for a broom to begin clearing up the mess, while Ernie took his friend to his own cottage for a cup of tea.

It's only a few flowers, Mandy told herself, and nobody even knew for sure whether they'd been upset by accident or on purpose. But she knew it looked bad. The campaign to get the caravans turfed out would latch on to just this kind of mystery.

'Do you really think it was them?' John Hardy whispered to Mandy. His studious face waited earnestly for an answer.

'No, I don't,' she said slowly. 'But try telling that to Mrs Ponsonby!'

She sighed and rode off. There was trouble brewing, and, if the anti-caravan campaigners got their way, the Riverside children would be made to feel even less welcome than before!

Six

By Thursday afternoon, Mrs Ponsonby, Mr Western and Mrs Parker Smythe had succeeded in rousing half the village into a state of outrage over a few broken flowerpots.

'Poor Walter Pickard!' Mrs Ponsonby wailed, buying her daily ration of mint toffees from McFarlane's. 'He cherished those geraniums!' Mandy caught the gist of her remarks through the open door of the post office. She was posting letters for her gran, before she headed home to help in the surgery.

'It should never have been allowed in the first place!' she heard Mrs Parker Smythe tell Reverend

Hadcroft. Mandy arrived home and propped her bike against the surgery wall, then went into reception. Mrs Parker Smythe and her daughter, Imogen, were coming out, as Reverend Hadcroft went in with his cat, Jemima.

'I don't mean to be uncharitable, vicar, far from it, but I *knew* the caravan site would mean trouble for the village. Why, only this morning I saw a whole horde of those children career past our house on those mountain bike things. And the two leaders are almost as bad as the children. They couldn't keep control of a kindergarten, never mind a bunch of unruly teenagers!' Mrs Parker Smythe was hard to ignore, in her brilliant turquoise dress and gold jewellery.

Mandy saw Imogen sigh and hold tighter to the cardboard box containing her twin rabbits, Button and Barney.

Reverend Hadcroft smiled back. 'I'm not sure that *control* is what it's all about, Mrs Parker Smythe. After all, the children have come to Welford on holiday. They're bound to let their hair down.'

'Oh, so you call destroying an old man's prize geraniums letting their hair down?' Mrs Parker Smythe retorted. She turned and seized the attention of Mrs Platt, who happened to be walking up to the surgery with her miniature poodle, Antonia. 'Did you hear the news, Mrs Platt? The caravan children were let loose on their bicycles up on the moor near High Cross. No thought of sticking to public rights of way, mind you. Oh no, Sam Western had to threaten them with his dogs unless they kept off his land!'

Mrs Platt looked worried. 'Things seem to be getting out of hand. I must warn Vicki and Justin. They're staying with me for a few days, while their mum and dad are away and I want to keep them out of trouble. You can't be too careful with young people these days.'

Mandy realised that Mrs Platt was the Simpson twins' great-aunt. She lived in a bungalow in a small modern estate and occasionally had Justin and Vicki to stay.

She watched Reverend Hadcroft ease his way past, and stopped for a moment longer to listen as the two women gossiped on.

'I felt so sorry for old Walter,' Mrs Platt went on. 'I saw him sitting on his bench outside the pub last night, poor chap, and he didn't look at all like his usual cheerful self.'

Mandy had heard enough. She gave Imogen a smile, and went inside. Her mind was still on the thorny problem of the Riverside children as she put on her white coat and went to help her dad with the vicar's cat.

'Ah, Mandy, I've already sedated Jemima, and now we just need to take a quick X-ray,' Mr Hope said. 'Lift her into position so we can take a picture of her tail; that's right. It looks as if she's done it some serious damage, I'm afraid.'

The vicar looked on anxiously as they carried out the X-ray on poor Jemima. 'I noticed her tail was drooping as soon as she came in this lunch-time. She wasn't her usual self at all, so I brought her straight here.'

'Quite right.' Adam Hope took the plate out of the machine a few minutes later. 'Look, Mandy, can you see a hairline crack across the vertebra here? About six centimetres from the tip? It's a fracture.'

Mandy looked hard at the X-ray, then nodded.

'It looks like Jemima may just have used up one of her nine lives,' Mr Hope told the vicar. 'She's had a narrow escape, by the look of things.'

'What will you do?' He stroked his cat and whispered gently to her, as she began to raise her head and take notice. The sedative was wearing off.

'We'll have to perform a minor operation to remove the tip of the tail. The fracture has paralysed the nerve supply. But don't worry, cats manage perfectly well without their tails. In fact, she probably won't even notice after a day or two.' Mr Hope picked her up and gave her to Mandy. 'We'll keep her in overnight and do the job in the morning, OK?' He told Mandy to take the cat into the residential unit and make sure she was put safely inside one of the cages.

Mandy gave Jemima five-star treatment. She put an extra padding of newspaper around the base of a clean cage, to stop her from banging the useless tip of her tail. She made sure she was warm and settled. By the time Mandy got back to the treatment room, Mr Hope had seen his last patient, and surgery was finished.

Now she had time to consider what to do about the Riverside problem. She told her dad about it. 'Do you think they're going round deliberately upsetting people?'

'Do *you*?'

Mandy shook her head. 'I think forgetting to shut Mr Western's gate must have been a mistake, pure and simple.'

'And what about Walter's flowerpots?'

She paused. 'I think the Riverside crowd are innocent until proved guilty,' she decided. 'I can't see that there's any concrete evidence against them!'

Her dad smiled. 'Have you thought about becoming a lawyer when you grow up?'

Mandy laughed. 'Oh no, thanks. Give me animals any day!' She wanted to be a vet, like her parents.' I think I'll just pop down to James's to see what he thinks.' She took off her white coat. 'And to see Henry, of course!'

'Of course. How's his diet plan going?'

'Pretty good. His weight's down to a hundred and thirty grammes. James weighs him every morning on the kitchen scales!'

'Excellent. Keep up the good work!'

She went off with a smile and a wave, thinking hard about how they could help Sonia, Marcie, Ben, Paul and the rest.

'What's up?' James asked. He'd been building Henry a playpen on the lawn out of four long planks and four bricks. The planks formed a square, propped in position and held upright by the bricks. It gave Henry a large, safe exercise area. He frolicked inside it as Mandy came into the garden.

'Mrs Ponsonby and Mrs Parker Smythe; that's what's up!' She flung herself on to the grass. 'They're dead set on blaming the Riverside kids for every single thing that goes wrong around here!' She told him the latest mishap with Walter's geraniums. 'I wish Mrs Ponsonby wouldn't jump to conclusions,' she complained. 'And I wish Mr Western wouldn't set his guard dogs on trespassers. People might not know they're on private property.'

James nodded. 'Have you seen anyone at Riverside today?'

'Not yet. I think most of them went mountain biking again. Has Leanne called?'

'I don't think so. I want to show her Henry's new play area. What do you think?'

'Brilliant!' Mandy began to smile. 'And by the look of it, Henry thinks so too!' The hamster was scampering from corner to corner, then sitting on his haunches and combing his whiskers. 'And I think he's actually *looking* thinner, James! You're getting him into really good shape!'

James smiled proudly. 'The extra exercise will help too.' He took a plastic dish full of clean water and placed it inside the playpen. Henry twitched his nose, bent his head, and trotted to the dish. 'Just keep an eye on Henry, will you, Mandy? I want to go inside and get a bit of hard-boiled egg. He loves it.'

Mandy lay full length on the warm grass, propping her chin in her hands, as James went off for Henry's healthy snack. His garden was lovely and peaceful. She could hear the bees buzzing from flower to flower, birds singing in the trees overhead. Lazily she gazed at the hamster as he explored the lawn for grubs and insects.

She looked up when she heard a faint new sound coming from behind the high hedge. Voices yelled, short and sharp. Someone or something came running along the lane in the afternoon heat. The footsteps grew nearer. Mandy peered through the hedge and caught a glimpse of a striped blue and white T-shirt. She raised herself to her knees to see who it could be.

The figure stopped running just outside James's garden. Mandy heard someone quietly sobbing, and then she saw a girl's face looking back at her through the green hedge. When she saw she was being watched the girl backed off and disappeared.

Footsteps started up again, heading across the road, then rustling through long grass towards a small wood opposite James's house. But Mandy had seen a flash of flaming red hair, and she guessed that the pale face and sob's belonged to Leanne. She sprang to her feet to follow her.

Out in the lane, as she checked the road for cars, Mandy spied two more figures heading towards her.

She recognised Justin and Vicki Simpson, the twins from school. They were walking Antonia, their aunt's poodle, but when they saw Mandy they hesitated.

Mandy frowned. From the grins on the faces of the pair, she guessed they were the ones who'd upset Leanne and sent her crying into the woods. By now, her blue and white T-shirt had vanished between the slender trunks of the larch trees, so Mandy turned to wait.

'Hi, Mandy.' Justin chewed the juicy end of a grass stalk and slouched along, hands in pockets. Vicki was letting the poodle strain at the leash. The little dog was panting and pulling in the heat. 'We fancied looking in on old Henry.'

'Feel free.' She cast a worried glance after Leanne. 'He's on the lawn.' She met Vicki's unblinking gaze. 'James has just gone inside to fetch him a snack. Don't let Henry out of his playpen, will you?'

Vicki tossed her head. Her bobbed brown hair swung back. Her solid, sunburnt arm reached out and pushed open the gate to James's garden. 'As if!' she retorted. Then she carelessly let go of Antonia's lead and the dog scampered across the grass towards the hamster's playpen. She had her nose to the ground and dragged the red leather lead behind.

'Watch out!' Mandy shouted a warning to James, who had just come out on to the porch with Henry's snack. James looked up, then leaped down the steps to head Antonia off. The poodle yapped. Blackie, shut up in the kitchen while Henry was out to play, set up a frenzied racket. Eric, snoozing on the mat, stood up, arched his back and hissed.

James zipped across the lawn like lightning. He scooped Henry out of danger, just as Antonia bounded into the middle of the playpen. Vicki charged after her, knocking planks flying as she seized the runaway's lead. Meanwhile, Mandy fumed at Justin, who stood propped against the gatepost, doubled up with laughter.

'It's not funny!' Mandy protested. 'And neither is upsetting Leanne Jackson. What did you say to her?' If she'd stopped to think things through, she probably wouldn't have challenged Justin, who liked putting people down whenever he had the chance.

'Oo-oh!' he replied. 'No need to get upset!' He stood free of the gatepost. 'We're touchy all of a sudden, aren't we?'

Mandy swallowed hard. 'No, I'm not. I just think we should give the Riverside kids a chance to enjoy themselves. Everyone gets on at them as if they were criminals or something!' Her eyes blazed. By now

Antonia's yapping had died down and Vicki had firm hold of the lead. She wanted to stroke the hamster, so James held him out for inspection. Henry seemed none the worse for his close shave.

'Well, according to my aunt, that's just what they are, a load of vandals,' Justin sneered. 'It's all she's been on about since we first got here. They wrecked a whole lot of old plant-pots, didn't they? And she says she bets the kids that come next week won't be any better, or the ones the week after that.' He seemed to enjoy the idea of other people getting into trouble. His lazy, lip-curling grin spread from ear to ear as he sauntered across the lawn towards his sister.

Mandy was still furious. She couldn't trust herself to stick around any longer. So she cut off across the lane towards the woods, knowing that now there was little chance of tracking down Leanne.

Sure enough, the sun filtered through the spiky, bright green leaves of the larch trees, the sweet smelling ground was soft and silent in the shadows, but Leanne had disappeared.

Seven

'Let's take Henry for a little walk,' James suggested that evening.

Mandy had been staring into space. She sat on James's garden swing with the hamster asleep on her lap, but she jumped at the idea. 'Down to Riverside,' she suggested. Henry woke up and shook his whiskers. He blinked sleepily in the evening sunlight. 'We could see if we can find Leanne and let her have a chat with Henry.'

The memory of the red-haired girl slipping away into the wood, her face pale and tear-stained, refused to fade from Mandy's mind. After the first, friendly visit, when Leanne had left the others playing football and come with Mandy to meet the hamster, they hadn't seen as much of her as they'd hoped. The shy girl had popped in once or twice with healthy treats for Henry, but the village gossip seemed to have affected her badly. She seemed to want to hide whenever Mandy saw her; in the village or strolling by the river. She still looked lonely and unhappy, and now this episode with the Simpson twins had probably made things worse. 'I wonder what they said to her,' she muttered, lifting Henry and easing him into his cage.

James locked it securely. 'Who?'

'The twins. To Leanne. I'm sure they upset her.' She told him about the running footsteps and the sobbing.

'Trust them!' James lifted Henry's cage and together they set off for the caravan site. 'Is that what's been on your mind?'

Mandy nodded. 'I suppose so.' They crossed the road and cut diagonally across the field towards Riverside. 'It's bad enough Leanne feeling she doesn't fit in with the Kingsmill crowd, without coming here on holiday and being treated like this!'

James agreed. 'Let's hope Henry will be able to cheer her up a bit.' They climbed a stile over a dry-stone wall into the field where the gleaming white caravans stood.

Chrissie Searle was the first to wave a friendly greeting. 'Hi, I'm just off over to Walton for barbecue bricks,' she told them. 'We're having a party tomorrow night. Would you like to come?' She stood, one foot on the mini-bus step, ready to haul herself up on to the driving seat. In the space of a week, the sun had lightened her short, blonde hair and tanned her long limbs. She gave them a quick grin. 'If you're still willing to associate with the likes of us, that is!'

Mandy grinned back. 'Just try and stop us!'

'Good. Seven-thirty tomorrow evening, then!' Chrissie climbed up and started the engine. 'See you there.'

The mini-bus drove off and Pete Cavendish came out of the camp shop. He strolled across, followed by a few of the children. Soon Mandy, James and Henry were part of the crowd. Marcie handed round her bag of crisps. Paul produced his football and began a game, while Sonia settled down and told Mandy a tale of being woken in the middle of the night.

'It was pitch black, honest!'

Mandy sat on the grass with Henry safe inside his cage, ready to listen.

'The dead of night. I wake up, and there's this *bump-bump-bump* noise right outside the caravan!' Sonia's grey eyes widened as she told her story, and her voice dropped to a whisper. 'I was scared to death, I can tell you! I dig Marcie in the ribs to wake her up. Leanne's already sitting up in bed wide awake.

'This thing, whatever it is, is going *bump-bump-bump* and the whole caravan starts to rock. I stuff the pillow in my mouth to stop myself from screaming. Even Marcie closes her eyes and clings on to me.

'But Leanne just gets out of bed, goes across and flings open the door like it's broad daylight out there! There are these huge, white, rolling eyes staring in at us. I think I'm going to faint. But Leanne starts saying, "There, there," and making these clicking noises with her tongue. By this time I've got my hands over my eyes and I can hardly breathe, I'm so scared. But when I take a peep, there's Leanne going for sugar lumps in the bowl and handing them to this *g*inormous thing that's snorting and breathing all over us. He's halfway up the steps by now!'

Mandy burst out laughing. 'What was it, then?'

'A giant horse! Grey. Well, sort of ghostly white in the moonlight. Apparently it had got in from the next field. But Leanne didn't turn a hair. She stroked its neck and talked nicely to it. Then she went off to take it safely back to its field. And the thing is, when she came back she was actually looking happy, like she'd enjoyed the whole thing!'

'Where is she now?' Mandy looked round, beyond the noisy game of football, towards the river.

'Who, Leanne? Don't ask me. She's probably wandered off somewhere by herself again. It's a pity, really. Me and Marcie, we think she's OK, only she's hard to get to know, she really is.' Sonia glanced down towards the riverbank and spotted something. 'Oh, there she is, daydreaming as usual.'

Mandy smiled and stood up, took Henry's cage and headed quietly for the river, as Sonia turned her face to the sun, ready for a spot of sunbathing.

Mandy didn't say anything as she sat down beside Leanne, who just gazed at the water which swirled lazily at her feet. Instead, she took Henry from his cage and settled him on her own lap. She began to tickle his ears with a blade of grass and waited for her friend to respond. Eventually, Leanne's gaze swivelled sideways.

'Hi, Mandy. Hi, Henry.' Leanne's low voice ended in a sigh.

'Hi.' Mandy handed over the hamster. 'Don't you think he's lost weight? James's diet is working really well.' She was careful not to mention the episode with Justin and Vicki earlier that day.

Leanne drew Henry to eye level in the palm of her hand. She nestled him close against her cheek. 'Yes, and he's still so soft!'

'And his coat is really shiny now!' Mandy agreed. 'That's down to the exercise and a better diet. We cut out all the starchy snacks that the kids used to give him at school.'

Leanne sighed again. She handed Henry back to Mandy and drew her knees under her chin.

'I have to go home the day after tomorrow.'

'I know. Will you be glad?'

'In one way. I'm looking forward to seeing my mum. But I won't see Henry any more, will I?'

Mandy hesitated. 'You could come back and see him,' she offered. 'Whenever you want.'

But Leanne turned away. 'I don't think so, Mandy.'

'Oh, don't mind what some people round here are saying!' Mandy wanted to put the record straight. 'Take no notice of the likes of Justin and Vicki. Whatever they say, we think it's great having you here, me and James, that is. And my mum and dad, and my grandparents. And James's family. We all like having the caravans in the village!'

A brief smile flitted across Leanne's thin face. 'But you haven't heard the latest, have you?'

'No, what?' Mandy stroked Henry and put him in his cage for a rest.

'Well, you know the tennis courts?'

Mandy nodded. 'Just over there.' She pointed a couple of hundred metres up river.

'There's a few new trees planted along by the riverbank.'

'I know.' Mandy pictured the saplings, carefully supported by thick wooden stakes and protected by a slim plastic tube around their trunks.

'Well, someone went along and snapped two of them clean in half. For no reason. No one saw it happen, but guess who got the blame?' Leanne turned to Mandy, her eyes full of anger. 'No, you don't need to say it out loud!'

Mandy groaned. 'Not again!'

'See. Whatever goes wrong round here, we get the blame for it. And those twins enjoyed rubbing my nose in it, I can tell you!'

'This afternoon?'

Leanne nodded. 'I was just walking down to James's house when they saw me and stopped me. Then, when they found out where I was from, they started yelling and calling me names.'

'What did they say?' Mandy went to stand at the water's edge. She felt ashamed and angry at the same time.

'All sorts of things. They called us vandals and stuff like that. They said to get back to the city where we belonged. And they said everyone round here hates us!'

'Well, we don't!' Mandy was steadfast. She tried to think straight. 'Anything could've happened to those trees. Just like Walter's flowerpots! I'll go home and ask Grandad; he knows all about what happens down at the tennis courts!'

Leanne tried to smile. 'Thanks, Mandy. But it's too late.'

'No, it's not. We'll get to the bottom of what's going on around here,' she promised.

'I hope you do. But what I mean is, it's too late for us. Too late for me. I can't come back to Welford and visit, see. Not after a week like this. I wouldn't ever dare to show my face again!'

Mandy poked the toe of her trainer into the clear water. 'Do you all think like that? Marcie, Sonia, Paul, and the rest?'

'Pretty well. Look, it's not your fault. Just forget it, Mandy.' Leanne stood up and ran a hand through her red hair, pushing it clear of her face. 'I only hope the kids who come to Riverside after us get on better with the people in the village. Maybe it's just our bunch that they don't like.'

'I doubt it,' Mandy shook her head, thinking of the fuss that Mr Western, Mrs Ponsonby and Mrs Parker Smythe would be making over the latest 'proof' against the caravanners.

'Well.' Leanne shrugged and turned to go. Then she remembered Henry and stooped to peep into his cage. 'Bye, Henry,' she whispered.

Henry twitched his little nose and blinked. He ran to the front of his cage to peer back.

'Do you think he knows I'm saying goodbye?' Leanne asked as she turned away, her eyes brimming with tears.

Mandy couldn't bring herself to answer. She watched as Leanne walked off towards her caravan, her own eyes filling with tears at the sadness and injustice of it all.

Eight

'Not a very good day for a barbecue,' Gran commented when she dropped in on Animal Ark the following morning. The sky had turned cloudy overnight, and a soft drizzle had begun to fall.

'Not a very good day, full stop!' Mandy stood in reception. She was wearing her white vet's coat and an unusually downhearted expression. Surgery wasn't due to begin for half an hour, so Mandy was keeping herself busy by tidying Jean Knox's desk.

'Why, what's the matter?' Gran bustled up the steps and put her shopping basket on a chair in the waiting-room. 'This isn't like you, Mandy dear.' She smiled a greeting at her son, Adam Hope, already at work in one of the treatment rooms. He was getting Jemima ready to go home after the successful operation on her tail.

'Hello there, Mum.' He came out. 'What brings you here? I was going to say bright and early, but it isn't really, is it?'

'Apparently not.' Gran was puzzled by the dull atmosphere. She looked curiously at her son.

'No use rolling your eyes and raising your eyebrows, Mum.' Mandy's dad came out with it straight. 'Why don't you get Mandy to tell you the latest episode in the Riverside soap opera? It's on daily, you know. It looks like you missed the latest dramatic instalment!'

'Ah!' Gran seemed to see the light. 'You mean the broken trees? Oh yes, I heard about that. As a matter of fact, Tom is down at the tennis courts right this moment, taking a look.' To make herself useful, she joined Mandy at the desk and began to sort out leaflets about booster injections against cat flu and other common ailments.

When the phone rang, Gran quickly picked it up. 'It's for you,' she said to Mandy, handing it over. 'Your mum's put the call through from the house.'

'Hello?' Mandy wasn't expecting a call.

'Hello.' A small voice spoke, then hesitated. 'This is Imogen.'

'Hi, Imogen!' She tried to hide her surprise. 'There isn't something the matter with Button or Barney, is there?' She couldn't think why else Imogen Parker Smythe would want to get in touch.

'No, it's not that. It's just that I wanted to say I was sorry.'

'What about?' Mandy gave her gran a puzzled frown.

'About my mum writing off to the council people again with that long list of names.'

'The petition!' Mandy's voice rose. 'You mean they've actually sent it off?'

'This morning. Does that mean the caravans will have to leave?' Imogen sounded upset. 'People don't like the caravan children, do they?'

'*Some* people don't,' Mandy agreed. 'But thanks for telling me, Imogen.' There was another long pause. 'There isn't anything else, is there?' She suspected there was something else on Imogen's mind.

'No. Yes! That is, can you come to my house?' The trembling voice sounded tearful. 'I need to tell you something else; a secret. But I can't say it on the phone.'

'Oh right, I'll try to later on,' Mandy promised. But her mind was on the petition. It seemed Mr Western, Mrs Ponsonby and Imogen's mum were really determined to get rid of the caravans at last. 'Bye then,' she said absent-mindedly, and she put the phone down.

'It looks like they're going to win,' she told her gran. 'I bet they've been collecting signatures all week. And now they'll say they've got proper evidence!'

Mr Hope snorted and retired to his treatment room. 'Evidence!'

'They will have told the council about the flowerpots, the cows on the loose up on the moorside, and now the broken trees,' Mandy continued. 'They'll say permission for the caravan site should be withdrawn because of all the trouble the city kids have caused.'

Gran's tongue tut-tutted rapidly. 'Well, really!'

'It's not fair, is it, Gran?'

'It certainly is not!' She tapped the sheaf of leaflets smartly against the desk. 'From what Tom says, it doesn't seem likely that even superhuman children could have broken those saplings. He says they were probably too strong to be snapped off like that.'

'Exactly!' Mandy agreed.

'That's why he wanted to take a look for himself.'

'Now, there's no point in you two just guessing,' Mr Hope warned from the other room. 'That would make you as bad as Sam Western's lot!'

'No way!' Mandy was put out. 'This isn't *guessing*, Dad!' Her fighting spirit was on the mend after her chat with Gran. 'Take the flowerpots; anyone coming out of the pub could've got into their car and backed into them!'

'Without even realising.' Gran was ready to back her up. 'Look, dear, what you must do now is follow up these theories. If you really want to help your friends at the caravan site, that is.'

'You're right, Gran!' With her head high, and a determined look on her face, she went into the treatment room. 'Dad, you don't need me for surgery this morning, do you?'

'No. Jemima here is ready for Reverend Hadcroft to collect. And Simon's due at any moment. There aren't many appointments in the book, I don't think. Why?' His eyes twinkled at her.

'You know why! I want to go and see Grandad. Then I want to go up to Beacon House to see Imogen. I think she might have something important to tell me. Then after that, I don't know what I'll do. It depends how I get on.'

'Get on with what?' He played dumb, his head to one side.

'With my investigations! I intend to find out the real people behind all this damage!' she said in a strong clear voice. 'It's wrong for Riverside to get all the blame. It'll ruin everything for the kids who are supposed to come here for their holidays this summer.'

'That's my girl!' A smile spread across Mr Hope's face as he gave her a quick hug.

Mandy grinned back and took off her white coat. 'Thanks, Gran,' she said, as she hung it on its hook. And without waiting for any more advice, she ran outside for her bike and pedalled swiftly down to the tennis courts.

Grandad stood in the drizzle, hunched up in his green padded waistcoat. He stared thoughtfully at the two snapped saplings. The cruel, jagged ends showed up pale through the mist. He looked up as Mandy ran to greet him.

'Hello, where's your jacket, love?' he asked, casting an eye at the heavy clouds. 'And what brings you down here?'

'I was looking for you, Grandad.' She tramped through the long grass. Behind her, the immaculate grass courts stretched, smooth as snooker-tables. 'I wanted to know what you think. Did kids do this?' She went and peered closely at the damaged trees.

Slowly Grandad shook his head. 'Do you want my expert opinion, love?'

She nodded eagerly. Her grandad knew everything there was to know about plants and gardening. He would know how hard it was to snap these trees.

'Well, I'd say it was impossible to do that with bare hands.'

Mandy took a sharp breath. 'Oh, Grandad!'

'I mean it. Just imagine, if you ever try to get rid of a strong shoot that you didn't want growing in your garden; a bramble or a stray sycamore. Well, it takes all your strength to snap something like that, and these two trees here are a good bit thicker than that.'

Mandy pushed a stray, wet strand of hair from her forehead. 'So what do you think could have done it?'

Grandad stooped to examine the ruined trunks. He sighed. 'That's harder to say. But look here, this plastic tube that protected the tree is split right down to the bottom, and there are scratches along the bark. I'd say that it was done by some sort of machine with sharp edges.' He stood up straight and looked up and down the riverbank, as if the machine could still be spotted there.

'A machine? What sort of machine?'

'Who knows? But if you think about it, it has to be a Land-rover, or a tractor or some such thing, to get down here. Yes, I'd say it was something strong and heavy like that. It must have caught the trees as it passed.'

'But definitely not kids?' she repeated.

'No,' he said. 'Definitely not.'

With fresh hope in her heart, Mandy waved goodbye to her grandad and shot off again on her bike in the direction of Beacon House. Grandad had promised to pass on his verdict to people in the village, while Mandy raced up to visit Imogen Parker Smythe.

'It may be too late to stop the petition now,' he warned. 'And there are those other incidents supposedly involving the Riverside children, remember!'

But Mandy refused to be cast down. As she cycled up the long hill, her legs aching, her chest heaving, she felt sure that this next visit would be another step towards clearing their name. After all, Imogen's phone call had come out of the blue. And she'd sounded shaky, as if something was bothering her.

Mandy arrived at last, found the security gates open and a black car standing in the drive. She cycled straight up to the front door of Beacon House, then rang the bell, glad to see Imogen's dad and not her mum come through the hall to answer it.

He opened the door. 'Hello,' Mr Parker Smythe said, surprised by Mandy's damp and dishevelled appearance. 'Have you come to see Immi?' He stood in a bright green golf sweater, one hand on the door, holding it half open. Imogen herself came bounding downstairs two at a time. 'Mandy's come to play!' she shouted, slipping in between her tall father and the door. 'I invited her!' She dragged Mandy by the arm into the tiled hallway and straight upstairs. At seven years old, she was small, but chubby and strong. Mandy felt herself being propelled into Imogen's splendid bedroom, complete with television, phone, shower-room and cuddly toys.

Quickly Imogen pushed the door closed. 'Oh good, you came!' she gasped, still refusing to let go of Mandy's arm.

Mandy stared at her red cheeks and secretive expression. 'Are you OK?' She felt herself plumped down on the embroidered white duvet on Imogen's soft bed. A giant black and white panda and a pink teddy bear toppled from the banked-up pillows and fell into her lap.

'Yes! No! Oh dear!' Imogen too collapsed on the bed, half in tears. 'I've got something to tell you, only Mummy will be cross with me if I do.' She bit her lip and turned away. 'I wish I'd told someone sooner, then they wouldn't have got into all this trouble!'

'Who? Who wouldn't have got into trouble?' Mandy tried to calm her down by speaking quietly.

'Those caravan children. They're going to be sent away, aren't they? The caravans, I mean. And all because of the flowerpots. And Mummy says they deserve it, and it's my fault because I let her think it was them, and then it was too late!' Imogen wailed and buried her face in her hands.

'Too late?' Mandy repeated. 'No, it's not too late, Imogen. You can tell me what really happened. You know, don't you?'

Miserably the little girl looked up and nodded. 'I saw. Mummy was in the post office buying a newspaper. I stayed in the car.' She paused.

'Go on,' Mandy said quietly. 'You see, it isn't fair to let someone take the blame when it's not their fault. You wouldn't like it, would you?'

Imogen shook her head. 'I never noticed the

flowerpots at first. I was looking at the cat.'

'Which cat?'

'Mr Pickard's big tomcat. He was sitting on the wall in the sun.'

Mandy nodded. 'That must have been Tom. Then what?'

'Next thing, the little poodle came running up to him. She jumped up. Tom hissed, and the dog jumped higher and higher, till it crashed into a flowerpot. She sent them all crashing down. Tom ran off and the dog stopped barking. When Mummy came out of the shop, they'd both run away. All the flowers were on the ground and the pots were broken!'

Mandy took a deep breath. 'And your mum didn't notice there was anything wrong?'

Again Imogen shook her head.

'Do you know whose dog it was?'

'It was a little white dog with a red collar. They shouted out its name. They called her Antonia, but she never took any notice!'

'Who's they? Who called?' Mandy frowned. These unknown people had witnessed the accident along with Imogen, but they too had kept quiet about it ever since. She felt herself grow hot and angry.

'I don't know. It was a big girl and boy. They both

looked the same. I think they must have been twins,' Imogen tailed off tearfully. 'Mummy drove away and I never said anything because I thought the big boy and girl would get into trouble. And then ... and then, everyone said it was the caravan children, and it was too late!' Imogen set about crying in earnest.

'Vicki and Justin Simpson!' Mandy let the truth sink in. Then she stood up, freeing herself from Imogen. She felt a small surge of victory; here was the first real proof that the Riverside children were innocent!

She went straight out and found Mr Parker Smythe still hovering at the bottom of the stairs. Mandy explained why Imogen was upset. He listened and nodded, then quickly took charge.

'I don't know much about this petition,' he confessed. 'I've been away on business for most of this week. But from what you say, it seems I'd better tell my wife what really happened to the flowerpots. It puts a whole new light on things. Leave it to me. I'll see what I can do,' he promised.

'Will you please tell Mr Western and Mrs Ponsonby too?' Mandy felt that things were working out well. Now she longed to race down to Riverside and tell them about the progress they'd made; the city visitors were in the clear over breaking the flowerpots and the trees.

'Of course.' He nodded kindly.

'And tell Imogen thanks from me, would you?' Mandy headed for the door. 'And ask her if she'd like to come to the barbecue this evening. She can come and join in the celebrations, all being well!'

Then she was off, down the long drive under the oak trees. She jumped on her bike, sped down the twisting road, through the village as the clouds began to lift and a watery sun shone through. She raced along the lane to the Hunters' house, brimming with excitement, hardly able to contain the good news. 'James will want to come with me!' she told herself firmly, flinging open his garden gate.

'James!' She ran up the path. The house was shut up. There was no car in the drive. Even Blackie was silent. Only Eric stalked across the lawn, his tail up and swishing from side to side.

That's odd, Mandy thought, halting in mid-stride. She spotted yellow flower-heads lying scattered over the grass, and one of Mr Hunter's flower-beds had been roughly trampled. Crushed marigolds lay on the damp soil, their petals strewn far and wide.

'James!' Now Mandy ran down the side of the house, to see if anyone was there. But the doors and windows were shut. Everyone was out and alarm began to dart through her. Who had come in and trampled on the garden? Was anything else damaged? She flew back round the front of the house and stared at the lawn, then slowly she went up the bottom step into the front porch.

'Henry?' Her voice caught in her dry throat. There was the cage on the shelf. But the top was flung open. 'Oh no!' She leaped the final two steps to look inside the cage. Henry's straw bedding was scattered loosely over the bottom, his drinking bowl had been tipped over, the sawdust was waterlogged. Even his exercise wheel lay on one side, and the ramp to his sleeping gallery had been wrenched out of position.

'Oh, Henry!' Mandy gasped. Frantically she searched every corner. But it was no good; the hamster's cage was empty. Henry had vanished.

Nine

'And you're sure you left the cage safely locked?' Mrs Hunter repeated. She stood in the porch, trying to understand what was going on.

James was white-faced. They'd searched long and hard for Henry since they'd arrived home from shopping, but now he stood and stared at the empty cage. 'Yes, I locked him in! I'm sure I did!'

'Yes, look, the lock's been forced open,' Mandy said. She examined the twisted bolt. 'It's not James's fault, Mrs Hunter. Henry didn't just escape. He's been stolen!'

James's mother put down her shopping and went to let Blackie out of the back of the car. The dog bounded up the steps and began to sniff around the porch. He gave a sharp bark. Then his head went down again as he trotted out on to the lawn.

'I think he's picked up some sort of scent.' Mandy tried to think straight. James's car had arrived just as she'd discovered Henry's disappearance. She had greeted them with the dreadful news and watched the colour drain from her friend's face. 'Blackie knows there's been an intruder, don't you, boy?' She had followed him into the garden, as the dog sniffed among the scattered marigold petals and the deep footprints in the flowerbed.

'But why? What's going on?' James sat heavily on the top step of the porch. He fought to control his feelings. 'Mandy, what am I going to tell Miss Temple when we get back to school? I can't tell her that I lost Henry, can I?'

'You didn't,' Mandy said firmly. 'Henry's been taken deliberately. Whoever stole Henry made a mess of the garden as well. Now, why would anyone want to do that?' She went to where the Labrador was sniffing at the deep prints. But her thoughts whirled without order. Henry was missing. The cage was empty. The flowers were trampled. But none of it came together to make any sense.

'And that's not the only thing.' Mrs Hunter sighed

as she swung down the back door of the car. 'We just drove through the village on the way back from the supermarket. There was a bit of a kerfuffle going on outside the pub. We stopped to find out what it was about. Apparently one of the kids from the caravan site is missing. Pete Cavendish was there trying to organise a sort of search party.'

James sat with his head in his hands, not reacting. But Mandy felt the hairs on the back of her neck start to prickle at the news. 'Who? Who's gone missing?' This was the last day at Riverside for the Kingsmill children. Everyone should be getting ready for tonight's barbecue, not spending time searching for one of their party.

'I don't remember the name,' Mrs Hunter eased past James to take her shopping into the house. 'Do you?' she asked him. 'James, Mandy was asking who they're looking for in the village.'

James looked up. 'Leanne,' he said quietly.

'I knew it!'

'She went off some time this morning and she's not been seen for hours. No one saw where she went.'

'Oh no!' The prickling sensation spread down her spine. 'Oh James, you don't think Leanne . . . she can't have, can she?' Mandy stared over his head at Henry's empty cage.

'You mean, Leanne was feeling so bad about leaving tomorrow and not seeing Henry again, and she was so fed-up and miserable about everything that she came and stole him and ran away?'

Mandy nodded. 'I'm not saying she *did*! I'm just saying she *might have*!' If you added things up, it was quite possible. She groaned. 'Why couldn't she just have waited an hour or two longer?'

Still shocked by Henry's disappearance, James got slowly to his feet. 'Why, what difference would that have made?'

'We could have got over to Riverside and told them the latest news. It turns out the Kingsmill kids had nothing to do with Walter's flowerpots getting smashed, and probably nothing to do with the broken trees either!' Rushing through the morning's events, Mandy told James what had really gone on. 'If Leanne had known that and knew that people in the village might not be so horrible to her any more, surely she would never have run off like this!'

'Maybe.' Mrs Hunter came out of the house with two cups of tea. She handed one to James. 'Here, I think you should drink this while I telephone your father at work. I want to discuss what we should do. I've already checked inside the house, and everything there is just as we left it. It's only the garden that's damaged, and of course, poor Henry.'

She left them to mope over the defenceless little hamster; short-sighted, over-friendly Henry, with his lovely marmalade coat and twitching whiskers. Where was he now? Was somebody taking good care of him? Mandy shuddered at the thought that the kidnapper might take fright and abandon him. He could be stranded in the middle of nowhere, unable to look after himself, and terrified.

'I only hope Leanne is looking after him,' James said miserably. His own thoughts had tended in the same direction.

'Oh, she will!' Mandy put on a brave face. 'Leanne *loves* Henry!'

'If it *was* Leanne.'

'Well, they both seem to have gone missing at more or less the same time. And she knew she was never going to see Henry again; she told me she'd never come back to Welford.'

There was a pause. They were at a loss, still swamped by fears for the missing hamster.

Then Mrs Hunter came bustling back. 'I phoned your dad, James. He says not to worry. We could always buy another hamster for the school.'

He shook his head. 'It wouldn't be the same.'

'No, but your dad was only trying to be practical. For instance, he wondered what was the point of the intruder trampling through the flowerbed. I must say, I find that very strange too!'

They all wandered across the lawn together to examine the heavy footprints.

'Well, it was no accident, that's for sure,' Mandy said. 'Someone's great big boots have stamped over here on purpose.'

'Your dad also said that if this Leanne girl is your prime suspect for Henry-napping, why don't you two go and join in the search for her? Better than standing around doing nothing.'

It took Mandy only a second to agree. 'Let's take Blackie,' she suggested. 'I'm sure he's picked up the scent. If we take him along, he can help in the search!'

So they went off down the lane, with Blackie eagerly snuffling and tracking a scent. They approached Chrissie Searle, standing at the entrance to the caravan site. She was poring over an ordnance survey map and directing Marcie and Sonia towards the wood where Leanne sometimes hung out.

She greeted them with a worried frown. 'Have you heard?'

Mandy nodded. 'We've come to help you look.' She thought it best to keep their suspicions about Leanne and Henry to themselves.

'That's good of you, thanks.' Chrissie sighed. 'Poor kid, I think she's been really unhappy here.'

'What do you want us to do?' James asked. He had to restrain Blackie by putting him on a short lead. 'Follow the others?'

'No, I've got this side of the village more or less covered. There's no real panic just yet. She's only been gone a couple of hours. But Marcie overheard her crying late last night, and this morning no one could get a word out of her at breakfast. Then she went missing. Pete and I thought it would be as well to start checking things out. We've been worried about her all along. She was too much of a loner, and now it looks as if something was really bothering her.'

Mandy nodded. She turned to James. 'Let's run on to the village, to see if there's anything we can do there.'

'Good idea.' Chrissie folded up her map, ready to set off up the hill after the distant figures of Ben and Paul. 'You'll find Pete organising things there. Half the village has turned out to help, much to our surprise!' With a nod, she set off along the public footpath, peering carefully to right and left as she went.

Mandy was surprised to see Mrs Ponsonby, brightly dressed in a daffodil-yellow outfit. She was at the centre of the huddle of people gathered outside the Fox and Goose, standing beside the tall figure of Mr Parker Smythe. Pete Cavendish, Mrs Platt, Walter Pickard and Ernie Bell were also listening closely.

As Mandy and James approached, they heard Mrs Ponsonby begin to hold forth.

' . . . So it seems, Walter, we may have been wrong all along!' Her rich voice rose above the murmur of all the rest. 'Most unfortunate, but all too true, I'm afraid!'

Mandy stopped and stared at James.

'Sit, Blackie!' he ordered quietly. In spite of their worries about Leanne and Henry, the opportunity to hear Mrs Ponsonby launching into a full apology was too good to miss. They hovered quietly by the side of the pub.

'If, as Mr Parker Smythe says, there are eye witnesses!' Mrs Ponsonby considered things. 'And of course, Mr Parker Smythe, we would never doubt your word. No indeed! We know very well that you

always have the best interests of the village at heart!'
She flattered and smiled, holding Pandora snuggled
under one arm, with patient Toby sitting to heel
amongst the crush of trouser-legs and skirts.

'And I'm sorry to hear that naughty Antonia and
Tom were the ones who were to blame,' Mrs
Ponsonby continued. 'You see, Walter,' there was a
teenie-weenie fight between them, and your poor
geraniums became the casualties of war! A pure
accident, of course. I know that little Antonia can
be a teenie bit wild at times, can't she, Pandora?
But I'm sure she didn't mean any real harm!'

Walter stood in his shirt-sleeves, scratching his
head. 'Aye well, Tom's always up to mischief.
And he's never been one to back away from a
fight.'

Mandy peered round the corner to hear Mrs Platt
offer her own, much quieter apology. 'If I'd known
Antonia had had anything to do with it, or that
nephew and niece of mine, I'd have been straight
up the street, knocking on your door with the money
to pay for the new plants,' she assured him. 'I'm
very sorry, Walter. I really am.'

'Aye well,' Walter mumbled again. 'It's all water
under the bridge.' He took a glance at his bare wall
and shook his head.

In the short silence that followed, Mandy, James and Blackie went forward to join the group. By now Mrs Ponsonby was gathering fresh steam. She fixed her straw hat firmly on her head and made a solemn announcement. 'The truth is out, and all thanks to Mr Parker Smythe's dear little girl, Imogen! And we have to be big enough to admit, each and every one of us, that we made a terrible mistake in making out that the caravan children were the cause of it all!'

'Blow me down!' Ernie Bell muttered. He gave a sly wink as he spotted Mandy.

'No!' Mrs Ponsonby raised her free hand to beg for silence. 'We must! Mr Western, Mrs Parker Smythe and I simply jumped to the wrong conclusion. And I know I speak for them all when I say that we wish to make amends!'

She turned with a swish of yellow skirt to face Pete Cavendish. 'To show how truly sorry we are, I can pledge that the whole village will stand by on the alert to help you in your search for the unfortunate girl. It seems she's a sensitive little soul, and our accusations may well have pushed her to the very brink before she decided to run away!' Mrs Ponsonby's voice had taken on a low, sorrowful tone. 'The very least we can do is to help to find her!'

Pete Cavendish nodded his dark, wavy head. 'Thanks very much, Mrs Ponsonby.'

'Not at all. Now, first we need a description!'

'Well, Leanne is fairly small and slim. She has chin length, red hair; lots of it, and she was wearing a blue and white T-shirt, jeans and trainers.' Pete filled them in on the appearance of the missing girl.

'Very good.' Mrs Ponsonby squared her shoulders. 'Pass that round, everybody! Now I must go and telephone Mr Western to inform him of the latest position. Ernie, you come along with me to Bleakfell Hall. We must make a thorough search of the grounds, leave no stone unturned. Come along now, everyone!'

Mandy and James watched poor Ernie's face fall a mile. But there was no arguing with Mrs Ponsonby. They watched the group disperse. Mr Parker Smythe promised to check the moortop beyond Beacon House, while Walter wandered off towards the pub to rustle up more help.

'We'll head down the valley,' Mandy told Pete. 'I know Leanne didn't usually go down that way, towards Greystones Farm, but all the more reason for looking down there, I suppose.'

'You may well be right.' Pete nodded his approval.

'Aren't you going to call the police?' James asked. He still had Blackie on the lead. The dog seemed upset by recent events, and was being even more disobedient that usual. He was whining and straining to be off the leash.

'Not yet. If Leanne hasn't turned up by teatime, we'll think again. But I'd like to make a thorough search ourselves before involving anyone else. We don't want to be alarmist; in the end we might find that she just wandered off for a quiet stroll. You know what she's like.' But though he sounded calm, he looked worried. 'Go on, you look down river, like you said. We'll all meet up again at four, back at Riverside. OK?'

Mandy and James nodded and set off. Now James could let Blackie off the lead, and he streaked ahead, down the path by Walter's cottage, towards the river. They could just see his black tail waving above the tall grass. 'He seems to know where we're heading!' Mandy said. They had to run to keep him in sight. 'Look, he's picking up that scent again!'

'This way, that's right, boy!' James said. They took a left turn by the edge of the clear water, and headed for the square stone farmhouse in the distance where Brandon Gill and his family ran their pig farm.

Blackie sniffed and was off again, loping along the pebbly shore, while Mandy and James kept to the narrow path.

Mandy seized a long stick from the bank and used it to swish aside bushes and undergrowth of poor-man's-orchid and willowherb. A strong aniseed perfume rose in the damp air.

'At least it's stopped raining,' James said. 'That's something, I suppose.' Then he drew to a sudden halt. 'Shh! Here, Blackie! Here, boy!'

Mandy halted too, while the dog charged ahead regardless. 'What is it?'

'I spotted something.' James crouched and peered through some bushes towards a clearing about fifty metres ahead.

'Yes!' Mandy saw a patch of blue, then red. 'Two people!' She saw Blackie race into the clearing, barking frantically. She stood up and sighed. 'Well, no chance of sneaking up on them, whoever it is. What's got into Blackie? I've never seen him as disobedient as this!'

James shook his head. They heard a boy's voice call. 'All right, James Hunter, we know you're there! Come out, come out, wherever you are!' The voice mocked them. Mandy recognised the jeering tone of Justin Simpson.

'Oh no!' This was the last person she wanted to meet.

'Can't you keep your dog under control?' he taunted, as James and Mandy emerged into the clearing.

'You can talk!' Mandy retorted. She felt herself colour up, as she mumbled a quick hello to Brandon and confronted Justin. It was Justin's red shirt that she'd spotted, and he stood now, swinging his foot at Blackie, who had crouched, alert and growling, just out of reach.

'What are you on about?' Justin hooked his thumbs into his belt and tried to outstare Mandy.

'I mean, *you* can't even keep your aunt's poodle under control!' she said angrily. She hated to see anyone trying to use their feet against an animal.

He realised in a flash what she meant, and turned to avoid her gaze. 'Who told you about that?'

'Never mind. But we know it was you and Vicki who let Antonia have that scrap with old Tom. Those flowerpots were down to you two!'

'Says who?' Justin bluffed, then resorted to insult. 'You're a right pair of little detectives, aren't you?' he sneered.

'Now hang on a minute,' Brandon cut in. 'No need to be nasty, Justin!' He looked puzzled. 'What's up with Blackie, James? He isn't usually like this.'

The dog had crouched low, ready to leap forward at James's command. He growled and glared at Justin.

But now Mandy stopped dead in her tracks. She forgot the flowerpots. She forgot Antonia and Tom. Her mind was focused on something completely new. 'Trainers!' she said in a faint whisper.

'What?' James held on to Blackie's collar and tried to calm him. 'What on earth are you on about, Mandy?'

'Trainers! Remember, Pete said Leanne was

wearing a blue and white top, jeans and *trainers*!'

'So?' James held on tight to Blackie. Justin stood his ground, feet planted wide apart, while Brandon frowned in bewilderment.

'It wasn't trainers that made those footprints in your garden, James! It was a pair of heavy boots!' She stared at Justin's feet. That was what had done it; she'd noticed the mud caked to his black boots as he swung out at Blackie. 'It wasn't Leanne after all!'

The sound of her voice, breathless and scared, set Blackie off again. He barked and strained against James, snarling at Justin, who still braved it out. Behind the bravado, Mandy thought she saw a flicker of real fear.

'Just what are you trying to prove?' Justin demanded. He laughed and jerked his head back in contempt.

But Mandy's mind was made up. Justin was mixed up in this somehow. That was why Blackie had flown at him; the dog had followed his scent all the way from the garden to this clearing. Justin Simpson was the one who'd trampled the flowers. And there was mud on the patterned sole of his heavy boots to prove it.

'Where's Vicki, Justin?' she whispered. Her gaze

flicked sideways to the gnarled and twisted trunks of the hawthorns at the far side of the clearing.

'Not here. Why?'

If Justin was involved, Vicki was seldom far away. Mandy turned to stare at him again through narrowed eyes.

'OK. So where's Henry?' She met his angry gaze. She managed to speak calmly.

Justin snorted then laughed. 'Are you crazy? That's it, you're round the bend, Mandy Hope!' He lunged at her, but Brandon held him off.

'Steady on!'

Justin wrenched free. 'Lay off, Brandon! Keep out of this! And you'd better not go spreading rumours about me and my sister!' he yelled at Mandy. 'You can't prove a thing, and I'll say you're round the twist! I'll say you set that dog on to me, Hunter! I'll tell everyone it's mad and dangerous!' Justin glared as he backed off from Blackie. Then he bent to seize a rough stone the size of his fist. He flung it at Blackie, missing his head by centimetres.

This time, Brandon flung himself at the dog to stop him from launching himself at the enemy. '*You're* the mad idiot round here!' he yelled at Justin.

Justin laughed as he scrambled up the bank

between the trees. Then he vaulted a wall, out of sight.

'Quick!' Mandy ran and grabbed James by the arm. 'Come on, you two,' she said. 'We've got to find Vicki before he does!'

'Why? What's going on round here?' Brandon demanded. He stroked Blackie's soft black nose to calm him down.

'Vicki's the one who took Henry!' Mandy cried. 'I'm certain of it! Come on, you two, let's try Mrs Platt's house. We've got to get there first, or who knows what they'll do to him!'

Ten

'Yes,' Mrs Platt admitted. Her face was creased into a worried frown. 'Yes, as a matter of fact, I think Vicki did have a little hamster in her room. I couldn't think where it had come from, but before I could ask her about it, Justin came back home!'

Mandy stood on the doorstep of Mrs Platt's small, neat bungalow, nodding breathlessly. 'When was that, Mrs Platt? Can you tell me how long ago Justin arrived?'

The twins' mild-mannered great-aunt thought for a moment that seemed to stretch to an age. *Please be quick,* Mandy thought. She had more questions jostling for position as she waited for Mrs Platt's reply.

'Not long ago. A few minutes, that's all. It seemed as if he was in an almighty hurry, banging doors and charging about.'

'And you say that he and Vicki went straight out again?'

'Yes. He dashed into her room with something urgent to tell her, I expect. Before I had time to turn round they were both racing out of the front door. I could hear Antonia barking out in the street. They didn't even bother to fasten the front gate!'

'Did Vicki take Henry, I mean, the hamster, with her? Did you notice?'

Again Mrs Platt nodded, then frowned. 'Oh dear, I'm afraid they've got themselves into more trouble, haven't they?'

Mandy didn't reply. Justin had beaten them to it after all. He must have cut across country from Brandon's place, across the farmers' fields, to reach the village before them. 'Do you know where they were going, Mrs Platt?'

'Oh no, dear. They didn't tell me. They were in far too much of a hurry.' Mrs Platt kept an eye on Antonia, who trotted down the path to greet Blackie. James and Brandon were waiting with him at the gate. Suddenly, she looked at them aghast. 'You don't mean to say that you think Vicki *stole* the hamster? Oh, surely not!'

Mandy nodded. 'That's what it looks like. Did you see which way they went?' By now, her heart was in her mouth. Justin must have told Vicki that they'd been found out. Now they were both out there with Henry, and probably about to do something desperate.

'Oh dear, now wait a minute. Yes, they went that way!' Mrs Platt waved her hand towards the main street, past the pub and the church, towards Riverside. 'When I went out to fetch Antonia back in I spotted them heading up the lane towards the caravan site!'

'Thanks!' Mandy gasped. She turned and ran down the path. 'They're heading for Riverside!' she told James and Brandon. 'And they've got Henry! Come on, we'd better hurry!'

Straining every muscle to catch up with the culprits, the three of them raced the length of the village street. James let Blackie run ahead. When he came to the sign for Riverside, the Labrador darted sideways through the gate.

'That's it, good boy!' James cried. 'Where are they, Blackie? Go on, boy, fetch!'

Eager as ever, Blackie wove between the smart new caravans. The site looked deserted; everyone was

out combing the area, looking for Leanne, so
Blackie's busy nose wasn't distracted by other scents.

'Why would the twins head this way?' Brandon
wondered. He paused to catch his breath just outside
the camp shop.

James bent forward to ease a stitch in his side. 'I
don't know. But you can bet your life that Blackie
knows what he's doing. They've got to be round here
somewhere!'

Meanwhile, Mandy went ahead, following on
Blackie's heels, praying that he was on the right
track. 'Go on, boy, find them!' She dropped on to
her hands and knees to peer into the gloom under
one of the caravans, then she backed out. Blackie
had squeezed through to the other side and was off
again, nose to the ground, tail wagging urgently for
her to follow.

She ran clear of the caravans towards the longer
grass by the riverbank. Blackie looked back and gave
a short, sharp bark. He stood, ears pricked, hackles
raised down the length of his spine. 'What is it?'
She ran up to him. He crouched down and barked
again, ran two or three steps, then returned.

'Show me, Blackie! Go on, boy!' Mandy whispered.
She followed the dog down the bank on to the
narrow pebble beach. And there Vicki was,

crouching behind a tree branch that swept low over the water. She looked wretched and afraid.

'Keep him off me, Mandy! Don't let him bite!' she pleaded. Heavy strands of hair had fallen over her eyes, but Mandy could see how miserable she looked behind the tumbled locks. She gripped the bough until her knuckles turned white.

Mandy stared. 'It's all right, he won't hurt you,' she said. She stretched out both her hands and spoke carefully. 'Vicki, for heaven's sake, give Henry to me!'

Tears began to roll down the girl's face. 'I can't.' She trembled and hid her face behind her hands. 'I haven't got him!'

Mandy groaned. She heard Brandon and James running through the long grass. They came to a halt just a few metres behind. 'You must have, Vicki. Your aunt told us that you'd got him. Now just hand him over, please!' She felt her nerves stretch to their limit. Her own hands were trembling.

'No, honestly, I haven't got him any more!' She looked up and sniffed, trying to pull herself together. 'But it's all right, don't worry. Everything's going to be fine!'

Bewildered, Mandy glanced the length of the beach. 'What do you mean? Where is he? What have you done with Henry, Vicki?'

'Listen, I want to tell you the whole thing!' Vicki took a step forward. 'Tell him to sit, James.' She waited while Blackie obeyed his owner's command. Then she came up close to Mandy. 'All this happened because I was jealous,' she began. 'When James was allowed to bring Henry home for the summer, I didn't think it was fair!'

Mandy clearly remembered Vicki's mutterings and dark looks, but she was impatient. 'Vicki, we don't have time for this! Just tell us where Henry is now!'

'I will, Mandy. But first, I want you to listen. You have to understand, then you can tell everyone what happened. I don't want them to hate me after all this!'

Though Vicki was tall and easily able to take care of herself, something about the way she talked got through to Mandy. 'Look, it's OK. If we get Henry back safe and sound, none of this will matter,' Mandy assured her.

'Well, he's all right. You've got to believe me!'

Mandy nodded. 'Go on, then.'

'It's just that I've always wanted to take Henry home, see. And when James was the one who was chosen, I just thought it was so unfair. James and you have loads of animals to look after already.

'Anyway, I sat around at home moping and getting

on Justin's nerves. Then when we came to stay in Welford with my aunt, he had an idea!' By now, Vicki was so keen to tell her version of events that she forgot all about her fear of Blackie. She laid one hand on Mandy's arm. 'We were busy keeping out of trouble after Antonia knocked over those flowerpots. There isn't much to do in Welford, just hang around, you know. Then Justin had this idea! "Let's kidnap Henry, if you're so keen on looking after him!" he said. He thought it would stop me moaning and give us something to do.

'His other idea was to make it look like the kids from Riverside were the ones to blame again. He said it worked pretty well before. I asked how and he said, "Easy-peasy. We'll go over to James's place and make a bit of a mess of his garden, make it look like vandals have been at it again. Then all you have to do is nick Henry from his cage!" He said no one would ever know it was us!'

'And you went along with it?' Mandy stared at her, open-mouthed.

Vicki's lip trembled and she nodded. 'I just wanted to look after Henry!' she whispered.

James came and broke into the amazed silence. 'Go on, Vicki. Never mind the garden. Just tell us what happened next.'

'Well, the thing is, Justin went a bit mad. He trampled everywhere, I couldn't stop him. He said he had to make it look like the Riverside lot had been at it again.' The tears rose again as she looked at James. 'I'm really sorry, James!'

He nodded. 'Is that it? You wrecked the flowers and forced open Henry's cage?'

'No.' Vicki took another deep breath. 'It gets worse!'

'Go on, you might as well spit it out.' Brandon climbed down the bank and offered his common sense opinion. 'Get it over and done with.'

'It's about Leanne, isn't it?' Mandy took a guess. Somewhere in the middle of all this, she felt that Vicki would be able to explain Leanne's disappearance too.

'How did you know?'

'Well, she's gone missing, and my guess is she didn't vanish for nothing. Go on, Vicki, tell us what happened next.'

'I was just lifting Henry out of his cage. Justin broke open the bolt with a screwdriver he brought with him. I thought we were going to get clean away, but just then the gate swung open and it was Leanne walking up the path towards us. You should've seen her face, Mandy. It was like someone had shot her.

She saw me holding Henry and she sort of gasped. She dropped a little bag of food she'd brought for him and she turned white as a sheet. She tried to grab Henry from me, but Justin got in the way and warned her to keep her mouth shut!'

Mandy pictured the scene; Leanne struggling to rescue Henry, Justin bullying. Two against one. No chance.

'Justin laughed at her. He said he'd put the blame on her when they found Henry missing! Everyone would know it was her because she was the one who was mad on Henry. He said everyone hated her anyway!'

Mandy's brows knitted together in a deep frown. 'What did she do?'

'She kind of crumpled, then she ran off. I just stood there. Justin thought it was funny, and he went off as if nothing had happened.' Vicki's voice trailed off at last.

'You know that Leanne's not been seen since, don't you?' James said quietly.

Miserably Vicki nodded. Her lip quivered again. 'I said I was sorry.'

Mandy wasn't sure that 'sorry' was enough. Leanne and Henry had both got the fright of their lives because of the twins, and they were both still missing. 'But you told me Henry was OK, didn't you? So just take us to him now.' She knew she sounded stiff and unfriendly, but right then she couldn't help it.

'OK, I'll show you. Come on.' Vicki led the way up the bank and through the caravan park. 'I did know that we'd done something really awful,' she confessed. 'When Justin showed up at Aunty's house, I said I wanted to take Henry straight back. That was after I'd had the chance to think about it. He was ever so mad. He said the plan had gone wrong in any case, and you'd found out the truth. I said I didn't care any more. I just wanted to put Henry back in his cage. I never wanted any of this to happen!'

'Is that where Justin is now, at my house?' James asked. He had Blackie back on the lead as they broke into a run across the field.

'Yes. In the end he had to agree.' Vicki began to gasp as she ran. 'But he said he would be the one to take Henry back. I'd only mess things up if I went along. He told me to wait here while he did it. He promised no one would see him if he was by himself.'

Mandy glanced at James. She didn't like the thought of Henry in Justin's tender care. 'Is your mum in?' she asked.

James nodded.

'But Justin would be able to creep up without being seen, wouldn't he? He promised he would!' Vicki insisted.

'Let's hope.' Brandon pulled up as he reached the gate ahead of the others. He pointed across the road. 'Here comes Justin now.'

They heard Justin's heavy footsteps on the tarmac. They saw him bend and shove something quickly into the hedge. They waited as he stood up and looked around. Then he spotted them. His face fell a mile. Mandy went to meet him.

'It's OK. Vicki's told us the whole thing,' she said to him. 'It doesn't matter, just as long as Henry's back where he belongs!' She longed for him to confirm it; that Henry was snug in his cage. Just those words, that was all.

He rocked back on his heels, scowling. He gave a short laugh. 'Tough!' he said.

'What do you mean?' Vicki pushed forward. 'Justin, you promised to put Henry back!'

'Too risky,' he shrugged. 'There was someone in the house. I couldn't get anywhere near without being spotted.'

'What are you saying?' Mandy demanded. 'Where's Henry? What have you done with him?' She still hoped against hope that Justin had taken the hamster back. 'Where is he?'

'How should I know?'

'Why, what have you done with him?'

Justin coloured up, but he hid his guilt with a final show of bravado. 'Didn't you see? I just dumped him in the hedge back there.' He jerked one thumb over his shoulder. 'So what's wrong with that, then? I did him a favour, didn't I? No more treadling around on that old wheel for Henry. No more being locked up in a cage. I put him back in the wild. I set him free!'

Eleven

Terrified, Mandy ran along the lane. Setting Henry 'free' was like passing a death sentence. He would be in immediate danger from foxes, badgers, dogs, cats. Even the stress of being alone in a wide open space might be enough to kill him. She stooped to rummage through the undergrowth in the hedge bottom, hoping that he'd simply curled into a ball until they came to rescue him. But there was no sign.

'At least we know he's still in there somewhere,' James said. 'He can't have run out on to the road, or else we'd have seen him!'

She nodded. 'OK, let's all go back into the field

and spread out to look for him!' She turned to Vicki. 'Will you help? We need as many people as possible. Henry won't last very long if we leave him to fend for himself!'

Vicki glanced at Justin, whose face was by now red with shame. He hung his head forward and shifted uneasily from foot to foot. 'Yes, we'll help!' she said firmly. 'It's the least we can do. Come on, Justin, you stand guard out here in the road. Let's get a move on!' And she led the little band of searchers back into the field.

They looked high and low. They searched under clumps of grass and inside hollows. They combed the field, they called his name. Brandon delved into his pockets and found biscuit crumbs. They tried to tempt Henry out of his hiding place by scattering them along the hedgerow. All in vain.

Then they enlisted help, as some of the others drifted back to Riverside. The unsuccessful search for Leanne turned into a search for Henry; soon half the kids from Riverside were ferreting through the undergrowth, underneath caravans and down the riverbank.

But by four o'clock, Mandy's hopes of finding the hamster were sinking low.

'He can't just vanish!' Vicki protested.

They gathered in a knot outside the clubhouse; Mandy, James, Brandon, Justin and Vicki, while the Riverside crowd kept on looking. Chrissie Searle had just turned up from the village shop with a hamper full of bread rolls which she'd ordered for the barbecue. She reported that there was still no sign of Leanne.

'Let's think; what would Henry be most likely to do in a situation like this?' It was James who thought straight as usual.

'He'd build a nest!' Mandy said. 'That's what he'd try to do. He'd look for dry grass, bits of sheep's wool, anything soft. He'd want a nice warm place, somewhere out of the wind.' She tried to plot Henry's probable movements since Justin had dumped him in the hedge.

'Now, now, we mustn't stand round idly chatting!' A loud voice interrupted them. 'Don't you know that the poor girl is still missing?' A bright yellow figure strode across the field towards them.

Mandy stifled a groan. 'Leanne's not the only one, Mrs Ponsonby.' Quickly she told the newcomer about Henry.

'Well, let's not waste any more time!' Mrs Ponsonby rose to the occasion with true wartime spirit. She rallied the troops. 'Twins, you take Brandon with you and carry out a systematic search inside the caravans! Who's to say that Henry, like any sensible little hamster, hasn't taken refuge inside a nice warm sleeping-bag or sock drawer?'

Eagerly Mandy nodded. 'Yes, we haven't tried inside the caravans yet!'

So Brandon and the twins set off under Mrs Ponsonby's command. Next she turned to Mandy, James and Blackie, the light of determination glinting in her eyes. 'And have you tried inside the shop? Just the place for a hungry hamster, don't you think?'

She took a few steps towards the door. 'Now, while you continue with the search in here, let me see how I can make myself more useful!' She rolled up the chiffon sleeves of her yellow dress, then turned to Chrissie Searle. 'Chrissie, my dear, I take it that the hamper contains provisions for tonight's barbecue?' Mrs Ponsonby didn't pause for a reply. 'Well, just carry it inside for me, would you, dear? My best plan is to press on with the food preparations, so that your little farewell party can go ahead according to schedule.' She marched inside with an air of hope and certainty.

Mandy's eyes widened. 'Do as she says!' she whispered. Chrissie picked up the hamper and turned after Mrs Ponsonby into the clubroom, while James and Mandy turned into the shop section, stacked with tins, boxes of crisps, shelves of biscuits and racks of fresh fruit.

'Isn't she amazing?' Chrissie said, once she'd deposited the hamper with Mrs Ponsonby, who straight away set to work with the bread knife. She sliced through the bread rolls with surgical precision. 'How can she be so sure we'll have anything to celebrate?'

'I don't know, but don't argue,' Mandy whispered. She dived behind the shop counter on her hands and knees, calling out Henry's name. Mrs Ponsonby had an eye on them through the open doorway. 'What are you going to do now?' Mandy asked Chrissie.

'Find Pete and carry on looking for Leanne. It may be time we got the police involved.' She looked serious as she went out and strode across the field.

Mrs Ponsonby had injected fresh energy into both searches. James stood on a chair to investigate the high shelves, while Mandy covered every square centimetre of the shop at ground level. Outside, the Riverside crowd still raked through the grass, while Vicki, Justin and Brandon carried on

examining the caravans. But still there was no sign
of Henry or Leanne.

Swish went the blade of Mrs Ponsonby's knife,
chopping down on to the cutting-board. She used
the snooker table covered with a sheet of thick plastic
as a temporary surface. The bread rolls piled high
on the table, as she lifted each one from the hamper
to dissect it.

Swish – chop – pause. Swish – chop – pause.

'Henry!' Mandy called softly, trying to entice him
out of hiding, crawling on all fours.

'Not up here,' James sighed. He climbed down
from the chair.

'*Aagh!*' A scream rang out from Mrs Ponsonby.
She snatched her hand away from the hamper, she
dropped her knife and jumped a mile. 'Oh my, oh
my! There's a rat!' She backed against the snooker
table. 'In the hamper! A rat! Oh my, don't let it get
out!'

Mandy and James sprang through the door into
the clubroom. They spotted stout Mrs Ponsonby
cowering against the table, her face and neck mottled
red, her hands clasped in front of her chest. Together
they dived for the hamper. They peered inside.

'It's not a rat; it's Henry!' James said calmly.

Mandy cried out in delight. 'Henry!' Unmistakably

him, with his cheeks full of breadcrumbs, his thick golden coat dusted with flour, his eyes twinkling.

'No, no, it's a rat, a rodent! In the hamper! I'm sure it's a rat!' Mrs Ponsonby's chins quivered. Her wartime spirit had evaporated.

'No, look,' James explained, as Mandy gently lifted Henry from the hamper to cradle him in her hands. 'It's a hamster. He has no tail, see. And rats are grey. Henry's golden brown.' He examined Henry's podgy cheeks. 'And he's just gone and ruined his diet all over again!' he declared.

Mrs Ponsonby peered more closely. 'Hmm.' She sounded doubtful. 'I'm not well-up with the anatomy of rodents,' she admitted. There was a pause. 'Perhaps you are right.'

'Oh, we are. It's Henry!' Relief brought tears to Mandy's eyes. 'You were right, Mrs Ponsonby! Henry did the sensible thing and headed for cover. He must have crept into Chrissie's hamper when she left it outside on the grass. Trust Henry to head for food!'

Sure now of Henry's status as adorable pet, Mrs Ponsonby moved in to study him. 'He certainly is a charming little chap,' she agreed. 'Here, Mandy, give him to me. Let me have a good look!'

Mandy took a deep breath. She could hardly refuse, she decided. Carefully she handed Henry over. 'Hold him gently under the tummy,' she said. 'Cup your hands a little bit more . . . oh!'

'*Oh*!' Mrs Ponsonby gave a little yelp and a shiver. 'He tickles!' She opened her fingers and flattened her palms, then took her hands away with a sudden jerk.

Henry dropped on to the table, landed on all fours, and took a surprised look round. Then he scrambled down the nearest table leg.

'Watch out!' James ran to close the door. Henry scuttled across the floor. He sniffed and twitched this way and that, zigzagging across the room.

'Got him!' Mandy cried. She almost cupped her hands over the top of him, but he darted sideways and vanished under the bottom of another, narrower door.

Mandy sagged forward in dismay.

'It's OK. I think it's some sort of storeroom or cupboard!' James seized the handle and turned it. 'It's locked!'

'No, I saw it open a crack. Something must be caught on the inside!' Mandy was right behind him, adding her weight. They pulled at the door with all their might.

There was a small cry as the door gave way. Someone stepped out of the storeroom. It was

Leanne. She stared at them, her face pale, her green eyes wide with fright, her red hair tumbling about her cheeks. Safe between her trembling hands she held Henry.

The full story came out, in the clubroom at Riverside. The search parties gathered happily, compared notes and congratulated one another. Apologies flew from villager to visitor. News went round that everyone was safe.

'And we're ready for the barbecue!' Mrs Ponsonby announced. She took full credit for assisting in Henry and Leanne's rescue. 'It was nothing!' she murmured. 'Really, nothing at all!'

Mandy grinned at James. 'It's mostly Blackie we should thank!' she whispered. 'Without him, we'd never have got on to Justin's track in the first place!'

James had delivered Henry and Blackie safely back home. While his dad fitted a new lock to the cage, James had weighed him. He was definitely a few grammes heavier, but content. The hamster was now fast asleep after his long adventure.

Mrs Ponsonby revelled in the happy ending. She reminded them once more of the barbecue, then pointed to an approaching figure. 'But wait, here comes Mr Western! Why, Sam, surely you've heard the good news?'

Sam Western stopped in the midst of the happy group. He was not a comfortable man. He cleared his throat. 'That's a matter of opinion,' he mumbled.

'Oh, come now, we've admitted our mistake. Mr Parker Smythe has telephoned the leader of the council to give his support to the caravan site. Let bygones be bygones, eh?'

Mandy saw Mr Western swallow hard. 'That's as maybe. But I thought it only right to come and tell you another bit of "good" news.' He surveyed his eager audience. 'I've just been speaking to my farm manager, Dennis Saville, and it seems one of my lads has been to him with a confession. He tells Dennis he took a Land-rover for a spin earlier this week, without asking permission. He brought it across country, down to the river . . .' There was a pause.

'Speak up, Sam Western!' Ernie Bell's voice growled from the back of the crowd. Half the village had congregated in the field.

'Well, the lad's a novice behind the wheel. And, to cut a long story short, he knocked into a couple of trees by the tennis courts. That's it!' He finished abruptly, overcome with embarrassment.

There was another pause. Then someone cheered. Soon everyone was smiling and shouting and shaking hands.

'And I'll tell you something else.' Ernie sidled up to Mandy. 'Walter's got his geraniums back.'

She thought he meant there'd been a miracle. 'That's fantastic!'

'Not the *same* geraniums, you understand.' Ernie tutted. 'Steady on. No, Walter's got new pots and new geraniums. Pretty as a picture, they look, standing on his front wall!'

'Where from?'

'From Mrs Platt. She thought it was only neighbourly, so she drove over to Walton earlier this afternoon and bought some fine new plants. She says the twins must pay for them out of their pocket money.'

Mandy nodded thoughtfully. 'You know, Vicki was really sorry in the end. And I think Justin was too, deep down.' She looked round, but they'd gone from the field.

'Aye well, they'll feel it in their pockets, and that's no bad thing, I say.' Ernie ambled off, saying that he might come back for the barbecue. 'Just to see what it's like, mind,' he growled. 'I'm not one for new-fangled ideas like open-air cooking, but I might just stick my nose in and take a look!'

The glowing faces round the barbecue that evening were proof of how well things had turned out. The clouds had cleared away, a full moon shone down.

Imogen came along with her mum and dad, James was there with Blackie. Brandon came early with his little brother and sister. The McFarlanes brought a free jar of toffees, the Hardys came from the pub with soft drinks. Bert Burnley, the farmer, had good news from the council leader. 'The caravans stay here at Riverside for the rest of the summer!' he announced. Adam Hope hugged Emily and led the chorus of cheers.

Mandy stood between her mum and dad, her face aching with so much smiling. Gran and Grandad were there to join the celebrations. The whole village was united again. And there was Mrs Ponsonby, the 'heroine' of the day, describing for the umpteenth time the part she had played in the rescue of Leanne and Henry.

'The poor girl had no one to turn to,' she explained to Walter Pickard. 'So she just hid away in the clubhouse, too miserable to come out. Apparently, she was absolutely convinced that she would get the blame for the hamster's disappearance! And then when I went in there to make sandwiches, she squeezed herself into that tiny store cupboard, poor child, still hoping to avoid discovery!'

Mandy listened. 'Just a second,' she grinned at her parents. 'I've had an idea!'

Adam Hope took a deep breath. 'Be warned!' he told the others.

Mandy sped across the grass to Mrs Ponsonby's side. 'There's only one thing I still feel sorry about,' she dropped in casually. She stared up at the starlit sky.

'Oh, what's that?' Mrs Ponsonby couldn't see any dents in the perfect conclusion.

'It's poor Leanne. She has to go home tomorrow, back to Birmingham. She can't keep pets where she lives. But she loves animals, she really does!'

'Hmm.' Mrs Ponsonby looked thoughtful.

Mandy rushed on. 'Of course, their school could keep a pet, couldn't it? I mean, Kingsmill would be able to have a hamster in their biology lab, just like Walton.' She sighed. 'I expect that's the closest Leanne could get to having her own pet. Only I don't think Kingsmill has one at present . . .' She allowed her voice to tail off.

'Hmm.' By now, Mrs Ponsonby's thoughts were

racing ahead. 'Would you excuse me, Mandy my dear. Now, where's that nice child with the blonde hair? Sonia, isn't it? Ah, Sonia, there you are! Just a minute, my dear, may I have a word with you?' And she trotted off.

Mandy grinned. Her stomach bubbled with excitement. It was her last wish for the evening; her parting gift for Leanne.

The Kingsmill School mini-bus stood at the gate, ready to depart. It was eleven o'clock on Saturday morning. The roof rack was piled high with rucksacks, all covered and tied down under a tarpaulin. The kids were piling on to the bus, while Mandy stood with James, who carried Henry inside his cage for a last farewell.

'Bye!' Mandy shouted. Ben gave her a thumbs-up sign as he parked himself on the back seat. Marcie waved both hands and grinned. Sonia climbed on next. She grinned over her shoulder at Mandy. 'I suppose the countryside wasn't so bad after all!' she laughed. Then Paul climbed on, with his football tucked safely under one arm. And, just as Leanne came to say goodbye to Mandy, James and Henry, Mrs Ponsonby drove her car into the field.

Mandy held her breath. Mrs Ponsonby got out and

opened the back of her car. She took a large, square object from the boot. It was covered in a piece of light, white fabric. Grandly she carried it towards Leanne.

'Now, before you say anything about this, I've checked with your headmistress on the telephone, and she's perfectly willing for the school to take Elizabeth. And she promised to phone your mother, and your mother has agreed. So, no worry on that score!' She held out the box for Leanne to take.

'Elizabeth?' Leanne frowned. She glanced at Mandy.

Mandy looked back, all wide-eyed innocence.

'Elizabeth the First,' Mrs Ponsonby explained. 'Daughter of Henry the Eighth, you know. Most appropriate. With a smile and a final grand gesture, she whisked away the cloth.

A pretty cream hamster with dark brown eyes nestled in the straw on the bottom of a wooden cage. Her eyes were huge and round, her ears neat and tufted. A band of white under her chin and round her neck shone clean and bright. She twitched her whiskers and blinked, then came forward to the front of her cage to say hello.

'Elizabeth the First,' Leanne repeated under her breath. She was mesmerised.

'I went over to Walton first thing this morning,' Mrs Ponsonby went on. 'The man in the pet shop says she's a good natured little creature, ideal for being with children.' She paused and glanced towards the mini-bus. 'There's only one teenie-weenie little problem.' Everyone craned out of the window to take a look at the new Kingsmill hamster. 'Who will take care of Elizabeth for the rest of the summer?'

Mandy thought she saw Mrs Ponsonby wink. Leanne was too busy gazing at the hamster to notice.

'Leanne!' they shouted, without a shadow of a doubt.

'Leanne should keep her!'

'She knows all about hamsters!'

'She's the expert!'

Leanne blushed and smiled, and tears of happiness filled her eyes. 'Thank you,' she whispered to Mrs Ponsonby.

Mrs Ponsonby put one arm round her shoulder and squeezed it. 'You should thank Mandy and James,' she said gently.

'Thank you,' Leanne managed to say. 'For everything.' She carried the cage on to the bus, and was surrounded by friends who all wanted a good view of the new school hamster.

'Thank you.' Chrissie leaned out of the driver's seat and smiled at Mrs Ponsonby. 'That was very kind. And we'll be back on Monday with a new gang. See you then?'

As the bus drove off, Mandy noticed Mrs Ponsonby take a lace hankie from her handbag. She gave a genteel sniff and dabbed her eyes.

'Say goodbye, Henry!' Mandy said. She waved them out of sight.

But Henry, back on his diet of lettuce leaves and dried oats, was hard at work on his exercise wheel. It rattled steadily as James and Mandy carried him down to the river, kicked off their shoes and stuck their feet in the cool, clear water. Mandy lifted Henry out of his cage and sat him on her lap in the full sunlight. He fidgeted, then curled up to sleep. She stroked him softly and began to daydream. The bright river flowed by, Henry snored. She was completely happy.

Dear Reader,

*I'm so pleased with the letters I have been receiving about **Animal Ark**. It seems there are lots of fans of the series, and I am very happy that so many people are enjoying the books.*

I especially enjoy reading your suggestions for new titles – so keep them coming!

Much love,

Lucy Daniels

ANIMAL ARK AS SEEN ON TV – LUCY DANIELS

70908 1	KITTENS IN THE KITCHEN	£3.50	☐
70911 1	PONY IN THE PORCH	£3.50	☐
70912 X	PUPPIES IN THE PANTRY	£3.50	☐
70913 8	GOAT IN THE GARDEN	£3.50	☐
71349 6	HEDGEHOGS IN THE HALL	£3.50	☐
70909 X	BADGER IN THE BASEMENT	£3.50	☐
71345 3	PIGLET IN A PLAYPEN	£3.50	☐
70914 6	BUNNIES IN THE BATHROOM	£3.50	☐
71346 1	DONKEY ON THE DOORSTEP	£3.50	☐
70910 3	HAMSTER IN A HAMPER	£3.50	☐
71350 X	GOOSE ON THE LOOSE	£3.50	☐
71347 X	CALF IN THE COTTAGE	£3.50	☐
71348 8	GUINEA PIG IN THE GARBAGE	£3.50	☐

All Hodder Children's books are available at your local bookshop or newsagent, or can be ordered direct from the publisher. Just tick the titles you want and fill in the form below. Prices and availability subject to change without notice.

Hodder Children's Books, Cash Sales Department, Bookpoint, 39 Milton Park, Abingdon, OXON, OX14 4TD, UK. If you would prefer to pay by credit card, our call centre team would be delighted to take your order by telephone. Our direct line is *01235 400414* (lines open 9.00 am – 6.00 pm Monday to Saturday, 24 hour message answering service). Or you can send a fax on *01235 400454*.

Alternatively please enclose a cheque or postal order made payable to Bookpoint Ltd to the value of the cover price and allow the following for postage and packing:
UK & BFPO – £1.00 for the first book, 50p for the second book, and 30p for each additional book ordered up to a maximum charge of £3.00.
OVERSEAS & EIRE – £2.00 for the first book, £1.00 for the second book, and 50p for each additional book.

Name ....

Address ....

....

....

If you would prefer to pay by credit card, please complete:
Please debit my Visa/Access/Diner's Card/American Express (delete as applicable) card no:

Signature ....

Expiry Date ....